Two Times Betrayed

Lynise

Copyright © 2013 Lynise

Published by:

G Street Chronicles
P.O. Box 1822
Jonesboro, GA 30237-1822

www.gstreetchronicles.com
fans@gstreetchronicles.com

This work is a work of fiction. The events and characters described herein are imaginary and are not intended to refer to specific places or living persons.

All rights reserved. No part of this book may be reproduced or transmitted in any form or by any means, electronic or mechanical, including photocopying and recording, or by any information storage and retrieval system, without permission in writing from the publisher.

Cover design:
Hot Book Covers, www.hotbookcovers.com

ISBN13: 9781940574066
ISBN10: 1940574064
LCCN: 1940574064

Join us on our social networks

Like us on Facebook: G Street Chronicles
Follow us on Twitter: @GStreetChronicl
Follow us on Instagram: gstreetchronicles

Dedication

To my boys...Isaiah and Richard. The loves of my life, we almost there. My mother Lynette; For always believing in me, and never turning your back on me. I pray to retire you soon and send you on an all-expense paid vacation. My sisters; Jelli, Bianca and DeDe, Still staying down even when I'm tripping. I wouldn't trade them for anything in the world, so blessed to have them as my baby sisters. My Uncle Derek, Auntie NeNe and cousin Mark (My partner). To my Bestest, Meke, love you girl for everything, and we gone ride till the wheels fall off. To my Grandma (RIP) Ana Pearl, My best friend (RIP) Blaimo. To everyone who tuned into "Deadly Friends" love you all. Hope you enjoy.

Last, but not least...Fresh, I wish we were better, I still love you and I hate that it ended up like this. Till I see you again...Muah!

Part One

G STREET CHRONICLES
A LITERARY POWERHOUSE
WWW.GSTREETCHRONICLES.COM

INTRODUCTION

Shasta's day-to-day struggle with trying to put her past behind her and raise a son by herself has begun to take its toll on her. In her mind, it seems like the closer she gets to starting a new life for her and her son, sooner or later, something or someone pulls her farther back. While trying to let go of a toxic relationship with her childhood friend Kila, the streets just keep calling her name.

Best friends forever is what Shasta thought she and Kila would always be. But as is the case in life, greed sneaks in, and we begin to learn who our real friends are—and they are usually few, if any. At the end of the day, family is all you really have—dysfunctional or not. This book is the first of many chronicles of Shasta Smithson; and although I'm classifying this book as fictional, Shasta's trials and tribulations are ones that many of us can relate to in one case or in a slightly different scenario. This book was written for all the women who came from the streets and thought that they would never find a way out. And to all the people who have interest in our struggle to survive…read with caution and please enjoy.

G STREET CHRONICLES
A LITERARY POWERHOUSE
WWW.GSTREETCHRONICLES.COM

Chapter 1

"Run bitch, we almost there!" screams Kila.

"I'm running as fast as I can wit these fuckin' heels on!" yells Shasta. "Do you see Ella anywhere?"

"No!" Kila yells back.

Kila approaches the door while fidgeting through her purse trying to find the gate card to the parking lot. Shots are fired. *Bang. Bang. Bang.*

"Come on bitch, they getting closer!" said Shasta

Another shot is fired; Kila drops. Out of pure instinct, Shasta quickly grabs the card off the ground, using Kila's body as a shield. She makes her way into the parking garage, running as fast as she can. She's filled with a since of satisfaction knowing that the garage door will close before them muthafuckas can get close enough to shoot her. Struggling with the keys, she manages to start the car; crying hysterically, she smashes out—hitting the steering wheel.

"How in the fuck am I 'bout to get out this shit?" Shasta says out loud while reaching for her cell phone. She calls her cousin, Nicko. Calling the police crossed her mind too, but she knew she didn't have answers to the questions she knew they would be asking.

"Please, please, please answer!" It continues to ring.

"Answer da fuckin' phone, cuz!" yells Shasta. Nicko picks up while Shasta is still yelling.

"What da fuck's up cuz? Where are you? We heard gun shots!"

Lynise

replies Nicko.

"Shit ain't go smooth, cuz; I'm in Groves Parking Garage. These muthafuckas tryna kill me. I shot one of them, but I think it's two more still trying to get in the garage. I don't know what to do and Ella isn't with me either!" says Shasta nervously.

"Slow da fuck down, cuz, we still in front of MAC'S spot, I'm on the way," says Nicko.

"Hurry da fuck up please, them bastards can't get in without a card, but I'm for sure they're waiting at the gate fa' me to pull out," says Shasta.

They both hang up the phone.

"What's up, brah?" asks Snoopy.

"Dat was Shasta, dem niggas got her trapped in Groves," said Nicko.

"What about Ella, she wit her?" asks Snoopy.

"Naw," replied Nicko. A few minutes later they pull up across the street from the garage where there is a clear view of the entrance.

"I don't see nothing brah, this shit don't look right. I thought you said we were posed to off 'em in da club." says Snoopy.

Nicko gets out the car and walks toward the door.

"Brah, what you doing, you gotta have a card; don't you?" says Snoopy. He hesitates to follow behind Nicko, but soon catches up. They see Kila stretched out on the ground—dead. As soon as Nicko and Snoopy enter the garage, Jason and Big fire off more shots at them from the gate...unable to get in. Nicko runs, firing back towards the sound of the screeching tires. *Pop. Pop. Pop.*

"I see Shasta," Snoopy says, staring in front of them.

Pop. Pop.

Nicko shots catch his target, hitting Jason in the chest. Shasta pulls up on Nicko and Snoopy and they both jump in the car.

"Took y'all niggas long enough," Shasta remarks as they get situated inside.

"It's one more nigga at the gate!" says Snoopy, trying to catch his breath. Shasta turns the ramp driving full speed in the direction of the gate; Nicko shoots out the front window. Big sees Shasta driving directly towards him, before he could move out the way, Nicko fires two shots to his chest and Shasta runs over him as he hits the ground.

"You got hit cuz," Nicko says.

Shasta looks down at her stomach and sees all the blood in her lap, immediately she goes into shock and crashes the car.

G STREET CHRONICLES
A LITERARY POWERHOUSE
WWW.GSTREETCHRONICLES.COM

Chapter 2

Almost Two Months Earlier...

The phone rings, Shasta tosses and turns in bed hoping it will stop so she won't have to answer it. It keeps ringing.

"Hello!" she looks at the clock and sees that it's 3:00 a.m.

"Who is this? Stop calling my fucking house!" yells Shasta. She hangs up; not able to go back to sleep, she grabs her robe and walks to the kitchen.

"Who is dat that keeps playing on my phone?"

She sits at her kitchen counter staring out the window, looking at the beautiful city lights. *I gotta get out of Atlanta*, she thinks to herself. Every since her and Chris broke up, she's been seriously thinking about leaving and starting a new life for her and her son.

"Fuck it, I'm just gone go. I can't take this shit anymore, ain't nothing left for me here, psf, sure as hell ain't no friends...fucking around wit Kila is bound to get me caught up one day. I'm getting to old for this street shit!" she says out loud; still talking to herself.

The phone rings again. This time it's Kila, not wanting to answer, Shasta can only imagine what Kila could be calling for this time of the morning. She answers, trying to sound like she's still asleep.

"Hel-lo."

"Bitch, stop flexin', I know you ain't asleep."

"Um...yes I was, I don't dance no more, bitch; why in da fuck would I be up this early? Ya know Lil' Chris got school in the morning,

Lynise

so whatever it is, the answer is, NO!" says Shasta sternly.

"Would 50 racks make you change your mind?" Kila asks.

Passing the floor, Shasta mumbles to herself, "This bitch always gotta play fa' something."

Fact is, her and Kila have been friends for a minute now, 'bout seven years. Kila was the one who started Shasta dancing at Loop's. See Kila was a real live hustler; she would do anything for money. Thing is, Kila didn't care who she crossed; it could be her own momma—if she caught you slippin', she was gone get you. She was also very attractive--slim, redbone, 'bout 5'6', nice C cup titties and a beautiful full ass to seal the package. So it wasn't hard for her to trick a nigga. Lately, Shasta hadn't wanted to fuck with Kila because of how reckless her name has been out here in them streets. At the same time, $25,000 could, and would, be the boost she needed to get her and her son the hell out of the city.

"Hello? Hello, bitch, did you hear me? I said 50k, what...you don't need no money?" asks Kila.

"You know I do. What you got up your sleeve this time?" Shasta replies.

"I can't talk over da phone. I'm downstairs, buzz me up," says Kila as she hangs up the phone.

Shasta pauses, getting a sick feeling in her stomach, she buzzes her friend up. The door opens and Kila bursts through it with a walk of authority.

"Pour me a drink, I gotta calm down before I spill da news 'bout this check," she says.

"You know where it's at, come on now girl, I ain't got all morning; what's up?" Shasta says with an air of frustration.

Kila walks back into the living room, staring at Shasta, with a little smirk on her face. Kila always envied Shasta, and she had good reason to. Shasta was naturally a beautiful woman. She had long, jet black hair; big, hazel eyes; and a body like a coke bottle. Everywhere they went, it was Shasta who was hit on first.

TWO TIMES BETRAYED

"Okay, bitch, this da deal. Do you remember them Memphis niggas dat came into Loop's the last night you worked?"

"Yeah, what about 'em?"

"Well, they got a spot up here now. I've been fucking with this duck ass nigga who be wit 'em and it seems every time I suck da nigga dick, he feel the need to spill da beans 'bout how they run their 'operation'…as he calls it."

"What da fuck does that have to do wit me?" Shasta impatiently asks.

"Freeze, bitch. I'm 'bout to tell you. So, okay…da nigga mighta fucked around and slipped and said Big."

"Who?" interrupts Shasta.

"Ya know, da fat nigga who kept giving you all dem $20 bills. I don't know why you stopped dancing, dem niggas be at da spot every Thursday."

"Damn it Kila, get to da point, it's getting' late." Shasta is serious, standing with her hands on her hips. Kila always jumped from one subject to the other when she talked to Shasta, by the end of their conversation, they'd covered damn near everything from gossip to weather. Usually Shasta would listen to her ramble 'cause half the time, Kila's chitter chatter kept her up to date on what da streets was sayin' and the other half of her ramblings were all lies; either way it went, Shasta didn't have time for Kila's shit this morning.

"Aiight, aiight. Now, what was I sayin'?" Kila gets up to make herself another drink.

"Oh, yeah, so da nigga was like…lately they been having a hard time cleaning the money, so they been keepin' it in da dog pins till da nigga, Dey, know he can get da shit funneled properly." Kila's adrenaline starts to rush from the excitement of potentially getting her hands on all dat money.

"Um, Kila, you know I don't fuck wit no dogs, and how you even know da money there for sure?" Shasta starts to gain a little interest in what Kila is telling her.

Lynise

"Girl, them dogs are for show; them fuckin' mutts ain't gone kill nothin' or let nothin' die. And as far as the da money go, he say it's more than that; it's close to a hundred thousand. I only wanted to get 50k so da dumb ass nigga don't get suspicious--they'll just think it was one of them that snatched it up."

"I don't know, girl, are you sure that money is there? I ain't trying to get caught up with them Memphis niggas." Shasta gave Kila her full attention now.

"Hell yeah, da fuckin' nigga got to my house last night smelling like straight dog shit, so either da money there, or he a fuckin' certified shit scooper," Kila laughs.

"Aiight, aiight. So when we gone do this…I mean what you need me to do?"

"Drive and watch out for me, I'mma go get da money since I be there all the time, it'll be easier for me to find it, plus da lil mutts no who I am."

"Okay, when honey? I'm down. Shit… I can use 25 racks right now, dat lil money can for sure go wit what I already have saved up. I can most definitely get out da city wit dat lil check," says Shasta with a ray of hope being released.

"What…girl, you still on dat move shit? It's plenty of money to be made right here in Atlanta."

"Well, you can have it!" Shasta says sarcastically.

"And I damn sho' want it…you just be ready in two days."

"Two days? That's fast, what's the rush?" asks Shasta with a cautious look on her face.

"Yes, two days. Time is precious. You in or out?"

"Didn't I say I was in?" says Shasta smartly.

"Well, it's settled then, Imma be back through round 9:00 p.m. Thursday; oh…and get a rental too." Kila got $300 out of her purse, threw it on the table, and headed toward the door. "Lata, Baby cakes."

"In the morning, Muffin," Shasta replies.

Kila blows a girly air kiss at Shasta and walks out the door. Soon

TWO TIMES BETRAYED

as Kila leaves, Shasta's stomach converted back to the same sick feeling she had before she let Kila in. Shasta had a serious bad feeling 'bout the events that were to take place in the next couple days. At the same time, she needed and wanted that money just as bad as Kila did. Maybe she wanted it even more, like the saying goes: *Scared money don't make no money*, and Shasta wasn't scared of going to get that money at all.

G STREET CHRONICLES
A LITERARY POWERHOUSE
WWW.GSTREETCHRONICLES.COM

Chapter 3

Today started as usual, Shasta made coffee while ironing Lil' Chris' clothes for school. He was four going on twenty-four, and he was the only man who meant anything to her these days. Normally, she would call her mom around this time, but today she decided to pass. She needed her head clear for what was to happen tomorrow, plus she didn't feel like hearing 'bout her baby sister, Candace, and her nothing ass baby daddy drama. It was cool out this morning as she got Lil' Chris ready. She threw on a nicely fitted jogging suit by PINK, grabbed her keys, her wallet, and her son, of course, and headed toward the door. Shasta knew she had a full day ahead of her and she wanted to get Lil' Chris to school on time for a change. It was only 7:00 a.m.; she had time to have breakfast with her son, so they went to McDonald's.

"Yea...McDonald's!" shouted Lil' Chris excitedly.

"What you wanna eat, baby?" Shasta asks. She loved doing things for her son. It gave her a sense of satisfaction. A feeling of knowing that in her son's eyes, she was perfect.

"I wanna eat chicken nuggets!" says Lil' Chris.

"Baby, they don't have chicken nuggets this early, how about pancakes?"

"Okay, when you pick me up make sure you have my McNuggets," says Lil' Chris laughing. Shasta laughs as well.

"Eat up, son. I don't want you to be late."

Lynise

"Talking 'bout how I am every day?" asks Lil' Chris sarcastically. "You too smart for your own good, honey!" laughs Shasta.

"I know."

Shasta arrives at the school twenty minutes later. As she walks Lil' Chris inside, she feels as if someone is watching her. When she doesn't see anyone, she shakes the notion off, and bends down and kisses her son goodbye as she hands him to his teacher.

"Bye, I mean…see you later mommy," Lil' Chris says, waiving to his mother.

"See ya lata, sweetie," Shasta says as she turns to walk away. She gets back in her car to see she's missed a call from Kila; a voicemail was left. The phone rings again. Shasta doesn't want to answer because she hasn't gotten the rental yet, and it is too early to hear Kila's mouth, so she decides not to answer the call and let it go to voicemail. When she gets the signal that another message has been left, she listens to it.

"I hope you got da car, call me when you get this. Bye."

"Told you," Shasta says out loud to herself. She checked her glove compartment to make sure her insurance papers were in there and she see that her pistol was inside. Usually she kept it in the trunk when Lil' Chris was in the car. She had forgotten to take it out and she began to get irritated. Traffic was the first issue of her morning.

"This is da longest fucking light ever, when da fuck is this shit gone change?" asks Shasta angrily to herself. She keys in the address to Nicki's Nails on her GPS – a new little salon Kila had been bragging about. She figured she could kill some time by touching up her nails since she didn't have to be at the rental place till 11:00 a.m. Shasta heads toward the salon when she notices a black SUV a couple of cars behind her. She would've sworn she saw that same truck earlier when she first dropped Lil' Chris off at school. *Maybe I'm tripping*, she thinks to herself. The SUV sped off fast in front of her.

"I hope you get there idiot! It's too early in the morning for dat Nascar shit!" She shouts loudly in her car. Ten minutes later, she pulls up at the salon.

TWO TIMES BETRAYED

"Good, I'm the first one in."

A little Asian lady greets her as she walks in.

"Color change," is all Shasta says.

The Asian lady quotes her a price, and Shasta takes a seat in a position where she can see the street. Shasta has always been paranoid for some strange reason. She is the type of woman that is always on the go. A few minutes later, the Asian lady is done.

"I like, thanks," Shasta says as she looks at her hair in the mirror. *What a pretty pink,* she thinks to herself. "Keep the change."

The Asian lady thanks her and Shasta leaves. Headed toward the car, Shasta sees the black SUV again; at this point, she realizes she wasn't tripping before. She grabs her phone as she gets in the car and decides to call Kila back. Before she pulls off, she gets her pistol out of the glove compartment and places it on her lap.

"Hello, 'bout time you returned my call, bitch; you get the car yet?"

"Freeze chick, I'm on my way there now, but that ain't why I'm calling. Girl, I think I'm being followed. I've been seeing this same black SUV all morning."

"Shasta, you know you paranoid as hell; it may be nothing."

"Nah, it's something…this muthafucka turning wit me, bitch!" Shasta yells.

"Where are you?" Kila sounds concerned now.

"Leaving Nicki's."

"K, well, meet me in ten minutes at dat gas station off da 20 exit, ya know 12 live up there, so if it's something…da muthafucka ain't gone try nothing up there," Kila says laughing.

"What da fuck's funny?" Shasta asks angrily.

"Nothing…just fuckin' wit ya, baby."

"Out of all the times you choose now to wanna fuck wit me? I'm ridin' wit Nina on my lap 'bout ready to pull over and give this muthafucka da business—who or whatever it is."

"Girl, you hell. Well, I'm here now; pull up."

Lynise

"What you driving?" Shasta asks.

"Red Benz," replies Kila.

Kila was constantly switching out cars; when Shasta first met her she didn't understand why. Over the years, as she got to know Kila better, she realized da bitch was into so much shit, she had to keep switching things up to keep niggas guessing. Shasta also knew Kila wasn't the perfect choice for a friend either; but they had a love for each other that no one would ever be able to understand. And the love they shared for da dollar bills kept them together through it all. Shasta knew one day that they would eventually go their separate ways, but till then, Kila was her girl. Her Ace.

"Imma park my car, I don't see da muthafucka yet. I think I lost 'em when I cut through Lee Street," Shasta says.

"Cool, I see you," Kila replies.

Shasta parks her car, puts Nina in her ready bag that she kept in the car for emergencies. She walks in the store and gives the clerk $20 to keep an eye on her car for an hour. As she exits the store, she walks over to Kila's car, which happened to be parked right next to a police car. She watches Kila as she flirts and throws googly eyes back and forth with the police. Shasta jumps in the car and waves 12 off.

"Girl, lets ride. Get a number and talk to his ass later," snaps Shasta.

Kila says her goodbyes and then pulls off. "Where to sweetie?" She blows Shasta an air kiss. Shasta throws one back.

Still irritated, she answers Kila while staring out the rearview mirror—trying to see if the SUV is following her again. She doesn't see it.

"Da lot, lets go get the car it's at the airport. Imma let Amber pick my car up when we get the rental."

"You are really paranoid, baby girl," says Kila.

"Better safe, than stankin' somewhere," relied Shasta.

"You right," Kila says.

Shasta goes through the CDs looking for the right music for the mood she is in. She wants to hear something gangsta. Who better

TWO TIMES BETRAYED

to listen to than her favorite rapper, Young Jeezy? She pops in Thug Motivation 101 as she reaches in the astray grabbing the blunt of purple that Kila had already rolled. She reclines the seat and gets her mind right. A few minutes later, they were pulling up at the airport.

"South or North terminal?" asks Kila.

"Um...South, I think. Wait...let me check. I got the directions on the conformation page in my wallet. It's South, Hertz got it."

"What you get?" asks Kila.

"A fucking Sebring, I think," Shasta laughs.

"Eww, naw, bae. I ain't ridin' like dat, I know dat ain't all they got," Kila laughs.

"Probably ain't! But shit...we gone hit a lick in the middle of the Bluff. Don't you think if we come through dat bitch ridin' a clean ass Benz, dat's gone bring too much attention to us?" Shasta asks.

"LOL. I figadilya," replies Kila.

"Soon as we done dat shit...it's going back ASAP, 'cause I ain't no Chrysler bitch. I have to stay in da best."

"Talkin 'bout I'm hell, you one ghetto sadity ass bitch if I ain't never knew one," says Shasta laughing. They pull up to the rental place.

"My reservation is for 11:00 a.m., its only 10:00 a.m., you think they got it ready now?" asks Shasta.

"They should, go see...Imma stay in da car. I'm tired as hell. I've been wit dat duck ass nigga all night. I think this muthafucka think I'm his girl or something," says Kila, laughing.

"At least you gettin' some dick, bitch, if I don't fuck someone soon...Imma pull my fuckin' hair out!" They both laughed at that statement.

"Girl, you a mess, go on in there and see what they say," Kila replied.

"Aiight."

Shasta walks in the rental company and approaches the front desk with an arrogance about herself. She didn't even notice that there were other people in line ahead of her.

Lynise

"Excuse me, miss," the lady standing behind says a bit irritated. Shasta looks back, glances up and down at the lady and turns back to the clerk at the counter.

"I have a rental reservation for 11:00 a.m. under Smithson," says Shasta. The clerk looks at Shasta as if she is an alien and says, "Ma'am, I would be happy to help you just as soon as it's your turn in line." Shasta pulls out a $50 bill from her wallet and places it on the counter.

"Can you help me now?" asks Shasta with a demanding look on her face. The clerk's whole expression changes; Shasta doesn't know if it is the money that changes it, or if the clerk justs wants to hurry up and service her so she can leave. The clerk looks as if she was in her early forties; small with a petite build.

"Imma be with you in a second, ma'am." Two minutes later, it was Shasta's turn.

"Welcome to Hertz. I'm Ms. Anne, what can I do for you?"

"I have a rental under Smithson," Shasta replies.

"Okay, let me check for you…a black, four-door Chrysler Sebring?" asks Ms. Anne.

"That's it," Shasta says.

"Okay. How long do you need it?"

"I'll bring the car back Friday morning," Shasta replies.

"There's a $150 deposit required, the monies are refundable back to your credit card once you bring the car back, and the rental amount is $86.39, which brings your total to $236.39."

"Okay, that's cool." Shasta gives the lady her credit card; Ms. Anne gives her the release papers to sign, then calls over the intercom to have maintenance bring the car to the front. Shasta gets the keys and goes outside, she see's Kila hanging out the window.

"It took you long enough…it takes two days to rent a car, I could've stolen one faster than that," Kila laughs.

"Shut up, bitch, you always damn complaining, and what da hell you hanging out da window fa'? Shasta says, shaking her head.

"Where we going from here?" asks Kila

TWO TIMES BETRAYED

"To yo spot, I gotta call Amber and have her go get my car too while I'm over there," says Shasta

"Okay, dats what's up," replies Kila.

Shasta jumps in the rental and follows Kila to her house.

G STREET CHRONICLES
~A LITERARY POWERHOUSE~
WWW.GSTREETCHRONICLES.COM

Chapter 4

Scrambling through her drawers looking for her black Armani Exchange outfit to wear for tonight, Shasta pauses to sit on the bed. *Is this what I wanna do*, she thought to herself.

"Fuck it," said Shasta. *It's now or never, I ain't gone let this opportunity pass me by. I need this money*, she thought to herself as she reached for her cell phone to make sure her baby sister, Candace, was going to be at her house by 5:00 p.m. to pick up Lil' Chris.

"What up sis?" asks Candace.

"Shit...can't call it; are you gon' be here ON TIME dis afternoon?" asks Shasta.

"I said yeah, sis!" replies Candace irritated.

"K, I'm just checking. Imma see to you lata then," says Shasta, rushing to get off the phone.

"Aiight, lata." Candace says before they both hang up.

Shasta knew if she stayed on the phone a minute longer, she would've never gotten off the phone, and the last thing she wanted to do is start her day off with Candace's problems. Shasta never understood why her baby sister always got caught up with these nothing ass, fake ass, wanna-be King Pins. She was so damn gullible; with three children under seven, and one on the way, everyone had just come to accept the fact that Candace was so smart, she was stupid. Shasta just did not have time for Candace's drama today. Getting back on agenda, she finds what she's going to wear and lays it on the bed. Since it is

Lynise

almost noon, she decides to do some light house work; as she walks over to the radio, she hears a loud knock at the door.

"Who is it?" she asks. No one responds and the knock gets louder.

"Who the fucks at my door?" irritation is in her voice.

No response, the knocks continue. Shasta looks out the peephole and sees a corny looking white man standing in the hallway holding what appears to be manila envelopes. She cracks the door open and asks the man what he wants.

"Are you Shasta Smithson?" he asks.

"Who wants to know?" she replies.

"I take it you are," says the man. He quickly shoves one of the envelopes through the crack of her door.

"What da fuck are you doing?" angrily, Shasta announces.

"You just been served," replies the man. He hurries to the elevators before Shasta can fully open the door.

"You fucking asshole!" yells Shasta as she walks up to the elevator doors and kicks them. Walking back to her apartment, she bends down to pick up the envelope and she opens it. The letter read, *Christopher Watkins vs. Shasta Smithson*, as she reads on, the madder she got. Her baby daddy was actually taking her to court for sole custody. She furiously ripped the notice up, saying to herself how much she hated his fucking guts. Pacing back and forth, all she could think about was her son. She would do anything to keep him and when she thought *anything*, she meant it. Immediately she calls her mother.

"Is this my eldest finally returning my call? I started to have Mr. Burrows bring me down there," her mother says.

"Momma, Big Chris is taking me to court for custody, he ain't did shit for Lil' Chris in almost four months and now he wants my baby? He thinks 'cause he done went and got married, he's a better parent than me!" yells Shasta.

"Calm down, baby," says her mother.

Shasta starts crying. "I don't need this shit right now, ma," says Shasta with tears running down her face.

"I know, sweetheart, when is your hearing?" asks her mother calmly.

"In three months," Shasta replies.

"Um, okay. Well, I have a friend who solves problems like these, I had to use 'em when dat nothing ass Carl tried to take Candace from me," her mother says.

Shasta goes to the bathroom to wash her face, attempting to pull herself together.

"Okay, mommy, I'm fine. I ain't gone worry about it. Imma 'bout to go put something in the air and try and calm down. I got some things going on today and I ain't got time for Big Chris's bullshit."

"That sounds like a good idea," her mother replies. They both give off a quaint laugh due to circumstance; it always shocks Shasta that her mother smokes weed too. Even though her mother never smoked with her, Shasta was glad that they at least had one thing they could bond over…especially based on the fact that their earlier relationship was like oil and vinegar.

"What time Candace coming for Lil' Chris?" asks her mother.

"She says round five, but ya know dat means six."

"Um hum, you ain't got to tell me how she always late. I'm still keeping Lil' Chris this weekend for you. Imma pick 'em up from school tomorrow, probably take 'em to the aquarium or something, but anyway I gotta go, sugar; *Criminal Minds* on, and ya know I can't miss a beat," her mother laughs.

"K, talk to you later then, love you," Shasta says, sounding a little bit better.

"I love you too, sweetie, don't worry 'bout a thing, let mommy take care of it for you. Kiss Lil' Chris for me too."

"I won't, and I will," Shasta replies as they both hang up.

Shasta checks her face again in the mirror; after approving her look, she heads back to the living room in an attempt to pick up where she left off before she was rudely interrupted. Her 2,000 square foot apartment in Atlantic Station was perfect for her and her son.

Lynise

Shasta fell in love with the high ceilings, but most of all, she loved her kitchen; to her that was the best part of her house. It sat right off her dining room and had a beautiful black centered granite island and matching countertops, with matching appliances and a built-in bar that separated the kitchen from the living room.

"Fuck the house work now," says Shasta. Rambling through her drawers.

"Why can't I ever find shit when I need it?" she asks herself. "Got weed, no blunts."

Although she was comfortable in her apartment—over the years she had made it a home for her and her son—she still couldn't wait to leave; she wanted that more than anything. Now that she no longer danced at Loop's, her nights were early, and her mornings felt so blank, she never had a so-called real job before, so even though she wanted to move, she still had no idea about what she wanted to do next. What she did know was that everything around her was telling her that it was time for a change. She just needed a way out; and slowly, but surely, she thought she was getting closer to that way out.

"I am so bored," she said out loud. She stumps through the kitchen to the living room and plops down on the dark blue cashmere couch like a two year old.

"Well, what's on T.V.?" Since T.V. was something she seldom watched, she didn't have the patience to sit and flick through 300 channels to see what was on, so she just laid back on the couch, and before she knew it, she was asleep.

Chapter 5

A black BMW pulls out the driveway, followed by a black Infiniti coup.

"Just like clockwork," Kila says. Shasta lights her blunt as she watches the last of the niggas pull off on the way to Loop's.

"Are you sure no one is in there?" asks Shasta.

"Damn it girl, I said no like a hundred times already. I even got Amber watchin' da club to let me know if Jason or any of them other cats pull out early." says Kila. "Either way, we ain't gone be here long."

"Good, da quicker da better," replies Shasta

"Okay, chick, let's get it…remember when you see da lights flash, dat means I got the money; all you gotta do is pull up on da side of da house wit da trunk already popped," said Kila.

A few minutes later, Kila was headed towards the back of the house. Since they had a camera on the front and side by the doors, she had to climb the neighbor's fence to get to the backyard by the dog pins.

"Fuck!" said Kila as she almost fell over the fence flat on her face.

"*Ps. Ps. Ps. Ps. Doggie, doggie,*" she whispers.

Two brown and black tiger-striped pits run up to her with there tails wagging. Kila pulls some treats out her pocket and feeds it to them. In delight, the dogs lick the treats off the ground and go to their own space away from Kila, leaving her to do her thing.

"Showtime."

Lynise

She grabs the trash bags she left out there the night before. Quickly, she pulls the side of the dog house out and begins to dig the dirt out with her newly-manicured nails.

"Jackpot!" she says with excitement. She begins to put the money in the bags.

"Shit, there's more than a 100k up under this damn dog house, nigga." she says to herself. Without a second thought, the greed in Kila takes over like a Klan meeting in the middle of Freaknik. Kila stuffs all the money in the bags, not leaving anything behind. She flashes the lights to give Shasta the signal that she has the money. Shasta pulls up on the side of the house—out of view of the cameras as planned. Kila struggles to throw both bags of money in the trunk; when Shasta hears the trunk finally close, she smashes off with Kila barely in the car.

"Go to da room," demands Kila.

"Which one?" asks Shasta.

"Fulton Industrial, I got one ova there," says Kila. Twenty minutes later, they pull up at the Airway Motel. Kila's car was already parked out front.

"Pull up next to my car and pop the trunk," Kila says as she gives Shasta the room key to go unlock the door. When Shasta enters the room, Kila follows behind, bringing in one bag of money.

"Didn't I tell you dis shit was gone be easy, bitch!" said Kila excitedly while dumping the money out on the bed. Shasta's eyes widened as if the sun was beaming right in her face. Even though she had seen her share of money, she never had seen this much at one time, and it was hers now.

"Kila this looks like more than $50,000 dollars," Shasta says nervously.

"It is, it was more there than I thought. Shit, bitch, dem niggas rich; they ain't gone miss it," replies Kila with a grin on her face. They both sit on the bed and began counting the money.

"$122,500 fucking dollars!" yells Shasta. "Hell, yeah!" they both reply, jumping up and down on the bed like kids.

TWO TIMES BETRAYED

"60k for you, 60k for me, and $2,500 for the lucky person who cleans this room in the morning," says Kila. Shasta stuffs her cut in the small Louis Vuitton duffle bag she brought with her.

"Imma let you drive my car home. I gotta stop to make after this and I wanna be discreet; we can switch back out lata."

"Okay cool, no problem" Shasta says. She really doesn't care what Kila has to do at this point, the only thing Shasta can think of is that she finally has enough to leave Atlanta. She grabs the car keys off the table; Kila grabs her bag as well. They both get in their cars and say goodbye.

"Lata, baby cakes," says Shasta

"In the morning, muffin," replies Kila.

Both ladies pull off, going in separate directions. They don't need the usual speech you see on T.V. about how not to draw attention to yourself. The simple fact is that they were already two bad ass bitches known in the hood for having a lil cake, and Kila spent money like she had fountains of that shit flowing out her pussy.

G STREET CHRONICLES
A LITERARY POWERHOUSE
WWW.GSTREETCHRONICLES.COM

Chapter 6

"It may not mean nothing to y'all, but understand nothing was done for me..." Jason listens to Drake on the radio.

"Where you headed to, brah?" Jason asks Black.

"My car ova my baby mama house," replies Black. Jason looks at Black, waiting on him to finish answering the question.

"Fool, which one?" laughs Jason.

"Ha, ha, ha. Funny huh? But fa' real doe, take me by Me-Me's, she on da eastside right off Panola," Black continues.

"Aiight." Jason says as he attempts to turn his music back up, Black interrupts.

"Loop's was whack tonight, I ain't even see ya girl in there either, and what was up wit dat ol' bitch up there, she had to at least be my mother's age, brah," says Black laughing.

"Hell, yeah, that's why I left Big and his freaked out entourage in there," says Jason.

"It's still early, what you finna get into?" asked Black. Jason's phone rings, its Kila. With a grin on his face, he holds his phone up towards Black showing him that Kila's picture was on the screen indicating her incoming call.

"I'm getting into this right here," says Jason with a lil smirk on his face.

"Sho' nuff, you stay fucking wit dat hoe lately, seems like you like da bitch or something," Black says.

"Damn, brah, it's clear that you don't like her. What da fuck she do

Lynise

to you? You get all amped up in shit ever time I say I'm going to go fuck wit her. You good, brah?" asks Jason grinning.

Black couldn't stand Kila, and Kila knew it. So did everyone else who grew up with them. Black and Kila went to school together back in the day, he used to have a lil crush on her, but she always turned him down. One afternoon during a cut party, Kila flirted and made little gestures toward Black as if she liked him. She did it just to get him to give her some weed. After all of the weed was gone, Kila ignored him for the rest of the afternoon till school was out. The next day, Black told everyone in school dat Kila sucked his dick at da cut party. Being the hoe that Kila was even back then, she flipped the story and told everyone that the only reason she sucked his dick was because it was too little for her to fuck. The two of them have been going at it every since, and when Black moved back to the Westside only to see that his boy Jason was fucking with her, it made things sour every time.

"Da bitch is just trifling, she told Neeva, my oldest little girl's mother, that I raped her, and she did it the same day I asked Neeva to marry me," says Black.

"Sho' nuff?" replies Jason. He thinks to himself, *ain't nobody 'bout to marry yo ass nigga.* He laughs.

"Hell, yeah, we were both fucked up one night in Loop's around the time when I first moved back to da Westside; called ourselves trying to put da past behind us and shit. I let da bitch suck my dick in one of da VIP rooms. When da bitch was done, she got up and kicked it like I was supposed to shoot her something. I would have, but it's how da bitch tried to handle a nigga that I didn't like. So I was like yeah, right bitch, you know what it is wit me, the next week da hoe went and told Neeva dat I raped her. She even went as far as showing her a fake ass police report and all brah," Black angrily says.

"Damn," Jason says, really not caring at all what Black has to say.

He knew there was nothing Black could say that would keep him from going to smash tonight. By that time, they pulled up at Me-Me's spot, and Jason missed another call from Kila. Black reaches in his pockets for his keys.

"Shit brah, just hit me up lata, I'm still finna go smash dis bitch," Jason laughs. Truth is he actually cared for Kila, she had a way of making niggas fall for her even though they knew she wasn't shit.

"Un, huh. You laughing now nigga, dat bitch right there is fucking poison, I'm telling ya. Neeva found out the police report was fake; but dat bitch still had my dumb ass baby mama convinced I did it," said Black.

"Aiight, nigga, I hear ya; but dat shit you screaming ain't fa' me; ain't no bitch ever tricked Jason, brah!" brags Jason. Black daps Jason down and gets out the car; Jason honks the horn as he pulls off.

Jason lives on the opposite side of Shasta in Atlantic Station; know one knew the irony of that living arrangement but Kila.

Ring, ring.

Jason looks at his phone, hoping it was Kila calling again. It was.

"Hello, sexy," says Jason.

"Hey, baby, how are you?" asks Kila.

"I can be a whole lot better if you come spend da night with me," he replies.

"Um, really? Well, lemme see what I can do about that then, where you at?" asks Kila.

"Just walking in the door," replies Jason.

"Okay, I'm at Apache' kickin' da shit wit my homeboy, Drique. Give me 'bout an hour to wrap dis up and I'll be right to you honey; is that okay wit you?" asks Kila.

"You need to be getting to me sooner than that," demands Jason.

"Ha, ha, Imma see you daddy; I got you. Promise," says Kila. Jason hangs up, three hours later he hears a knock at the door.

"Who is it?" yells Jason.

"Come and see," says Kila.

Jason looks at his watch. "You late!" he yells. Jason opens the door to see Kila standing there in an all-black see-through mini dress. She had her long hair pinned up in a bun. He couldn't help but notice how fine

Lynise

she was; her being three hours late didn't seem to bother him anymore. "You gone invite me in, or is you gone stand there and stare?" asks Kila grinning. Jason quickly moves aside for Kila to enter.

"Lead da way, sexy…mmm." Jason says with his hand on his dick as he follows behind her.

"What you got to drink?" she asks as she throws her purse on the table and heads to the kitchen with Jason still tailing her every move.

"There's still some Hen in there from the other night you was here… in da cabinet," he replies. Kila takes out two glasses and grabs the sack she had stuffed down in her pocket, she pours her and Jason a drink.

"You want a one on one?" asks Kila.

"You know I don't fuck wit dat shit girl; but I got some more fa' ya if you run out." "I know you don't, honey, but you don't know what you're missing," she says with a smile.

Jason watches as Kila does a few lines, and he notices she's missing one of the earrings he bought her last week.

"Where yo' other earring at ma?"

Kila feels her ears and notices one is missing as well.

"Oh, shit baby, it must've come off when I was fixin' my hair in the car before I came up."

"Damn, baby, I spent a gwap on those earrings; how you gone make dat up to me?" asks Jason as he walks over to Kila.

"Oh, yeah, what I gotta do then, daddy," says Kila as she gets closer to Jason. She slowly takes off her dress, leaving her black thong on.

"Umph, umph, umph," says Jason.

"What…you like?" asks Kila as she spends around for Jason to get a full view.

"Hell, yeah," replies Jason.

He picks Kila up and places her on the counter, and begins kissing and caressing her nipples. Kila uses her feet to push his jogging pants to the floor. Jason lifts her legs up and puts his pleasure inside of her. Not able to hold his balance, he pick her up with him still inside of her and finishes fucking Kila on the kitchen floor.

Chapter 7

Shasta hated picking up Lil' Chris from Candace's house. Out of all the places she could've used her Section 8 to live, she moved right on Hollywood Road. Now don't get it twisted, Shasta was from Perry Holmes, and before she started making money and jugging out of Loop's, she had an apartment in Flipper Temple. Candace was another story, she is like a white person stuck in a black body with ghetto tendencies. She is clueless, on every aspect, when it comes to da streets. Candace only moved there because that's where baby daddy number four was from. It is like she is trying to be a part of a lifestyle that just doesn't fit her. The sad part is that no one thinks she will ever realize that, at least not right now.

Shasta pulls in front of Candace's house, right across from Scott Elementary School. She honks the horn, not wanting to get out.

"Bonk, Bonk!"

Shasta honks repeatedly. A dark-skinned young male looks out the door.

"It's a red Benz out here!" yells the boy.

Irritated, Shasta grabs her cell phone to call Candace, but sees her hanging out the window instead.

"Why you don't get out, sis?" asks Candace.

Shasta loves her sister, but hates the latest boyfriend. She and Candace used to kick it wit each other at least three or four times a week before she got with his ass.

Lynise

"I'm sleepy, baby girl; maybe another day. Is my baby ready?" asks Shasta.

"Yeah, but he is asleep though, Imma bring him out to ya."

A few minutes later, Candace brought Lil' Chris out to the car.

"I see you and Kila still trading cars," says Candace smiling.

"Yeah, you know how she is," replies Shasta.

"Uh huh, dat I do. She's sneaky, trifling, and ain't no way in the hell I would still be friends with her if she fucked my baby daddy," said Candace, shaking her head in true belief of everything she just said to her sister.

"Which fucking one? You don't know dat fa' sure, those were just rumors anyway!" said Shasta angrily, she hated it when people said things to her about Kila. She felt it was up to her to choose her friends, no matter how much everyone agreed in their feelings for Kila.

"Rumors my ass. I may not be as street smart as you honey, but one thing I do know is when a nigga fuckin' off, and dat bitch Kila was fucking Big Chris. Everyone knew it except for you. I guess Miss high and mighty been bit by da stupid bug too, just like da rest of us women have," Candace replies.

"What fucking bug, bitch? You tripping," Shasta replies with anger in her voice.

"Dah...I was stupid fa' a nigga too. That shit runs through da family," laughs Candace. Shasta grabs her wallet, took out $200 and throws it out the passenger window at Candace and smashed off.

"Bitch!" yells Candace as she bends down to pick the money up off the ground.

Shasta can't wait to get home, today's events have taken a lot out of her. All she wants to do is go home, relax and pack; yet the only thing that seems to calm her is that she knows that she is $60,000 richer than she was this morning.

"Home at last," says Shasta. She grabs Lil' Chris, her things out of the car and proceeds to the elevators. Keys drop. Shasta turns around to see where the noise is coming from, and she sees nobody. Keys

TWO TIMES BETRAYED

drop again, Shasta gets the same bad feeling she had this morning when she was being followed. She fondles through her bag hoping she got Nina out of the car while trying to hold Lil' Chris up.

"What da fucks up with these elevators?" asks Shasta, talking to herself. She presses the button for the operator and gets no answer. She turns in the direction of the stairs, but is immediately blinded by bright lights. She throws her hands up to kind of block the light so she can get a glimpse of the driver, but all she sees is the color of the vehicle. It's a black SUV, like the one from earlier. Shasta figures the truck has to have been sitting there parked, because she didn't hear or see another vehicle come up behind her. Shasta starts pushing the elevator buttons again, she thinks about taking the stairs, but she lived on the fifteenth floor, and with Lil' Chris still being asleep, she can't see herself getting up that many flights safely; plus, she wants to stay out in the open.

"Damn it! Open fucking up, all this money I pay for this condo and the elevators don't wanna work!" yells Shasta as she kicks the elevator doors.

"Lil' Chris…baby, baby, wake up honey," says Shasta.

"Maaa," moans Lil' Chris.

"Let's play a game, ok, honey," says Shasta, still looking through her bag as she realizes that she left her gun in the rental with Kila. The only thing she can think to do now is make a scene and hope someone will hear her if the person behind her decided to get out of the car. She pushes the alarm on Kila's car, it lets off an annoying sound. The SUV appears to be getting closer, she really can't tell because of how bright the lights are. A man's voice comes over the intercom.

"Can I help you, miss?" asks the man.

"Why in the fuck aren't the elevators working? I need security down hear now!" yells Shasta.

"You have to use your card after midnight, ma'am."

Shasta knew that, but that too was in the other car.

"Look, I don't have my card, I live on the fifteenth floor, apartment

Lynise

1508. My name is Shasta Smithson, I have my son out here and he does not feel good...open da fucking elevators or you won't have a fucking job to come back to tomorrow!" Shasta yells.

A few seconds later, she gets on the elevator with bright lights still flashing at her. Shasta got off on the eighteenth floor just in case *Mr. Psycho* was still downstairs in the parking lot watching to see what floor she lives on.

"Is this the game, mommy?" asks Lil' Chris.

"Yes, it is sweetie, let's see how fast you can run down these steps. Whoever reaches our apartment first is the winner." Shasta says as Lil' Chris takes off with Shasta right behind him.

Chapter 8

Buzz. Buzz. Buzz. Buzz.

Big presses the intercom to Jason's apartment.

"Call his phone, cuz," says Big.

"I am, it's going straight to voicemail," says Black.

Big presses the buzzer again. This time Jason answers.

"Yo', who dat keep pressin' da damn buzzer?" asks Jason.

"It's Big nigga, come down," replies Big. Jason hears Black's voice in the background as well.

"Y'all niggas don't know what a phone do, instead ringing dat irritating ass intercom like dat?" asks Jason.

"Man, me and Black been calling yo' ass all weekend, check yo' cheap ass phone…dat shit been going to voicemail. Anyway nigga, come down, we got some business to take care of this morning," Big replies.

"Aiight, aiight. Imma be down in a sec, let me wash my face and shit," Jason says. A few minutes later, Jason gets off the elevator. Big is sitting in the lobby talking on his cell phone, and Black is at the desk flirting with the receptionist.

"Ms. Sheila, don't fuck wit dat nigga," says Jason grinning. Ms. Sheila smiles at Jason while holding up her hand to show off her wedding ring.

"Ha, ha, ha, no worries, honey, you know I LOVE my husband," says Ms. Sheila while looking Black dead in his eyes as she makes

Lynise

her comment. Black winks back at Ms. Sheila letting her know that he didn't care 'bout the ring she was flashing.

"Gone now, honey, I'm good." She turns to pretend she was busy, and Black walks off toward Big and Jason.

"What up, brah?" asks Big. He daps down Jason and so did Black.

"Shit…same ol'…so what we got on the agenda for today, brah?" asks Jason.

"I just got off the phone wit Mr. Iman, he says he's ready for us. We gotta move the money today if we plan on being right lata," says Big.

Big and Jason are the brains in the operation; the money they are making they know will only last for so long. So about a year ago, they decided to open up a club together in case shit hit the fan on the streets they would have receipts for the lifestyles they were living. Plus, they knew two niggas walking in a bank with a half million dollars was not the move to make. Black, on the other hand, was the real definition of a street nigga. His plan was to sell drugs until they stop producing them, even though getting rid of a nigga was his talent most known on the streets. Every street team either had a nigga like Black down or needed a nigga like Black down.

"Brah, why you ain't been answering ya phone, you know fine ass Cece threw a party Saturday at Dancer's Elite. It was so many fine ass hoes in there, dat bitch Pinky, who be on dem flicks, even came through and showed some love to a nigga, and she fine as hell too," Black says.

"Man, stop flexin'. You fa' get I was there too, and to my memory, dat broad wasn't paying yo' ass no attention," Big laughs. Jason shakes his head in laughter as well.

"Shit, anyway my nigga, I stayed in this weekend," Jason replies. Big studied Black's face after Jason's last statement.

"Uh, huh, I noticed you been M.I.A. lately; don't tell me you actually trying to make something wit dat bitch Kila?" asks Big. Big didn't have no beef with Kila, he may have fucked her once or twice, but there was no bad blood between them.

"There you go, I see Black got you dat same shit he on now, huh. Tell me dis, did I say anything to you, when yo' ass went and married dat hood rat bitch, Monica, last year in Vegas. Hell, you ain't even know da hoe one week; y'all was politican at da Mexican Bar, da next week you were flying her out to Vegas. At least I know Kila, you still getting to know your so-called wife. Hell, is her name really Monica, brah?" laughs Jason.

Black busts out laughing too. Big cuts his eyes at him and Jason stops laughing.

"Ya, ya, anyway nigga, yo' ass betta be careful when it comes to Kila, dat bitch is poison let everyone else tell it," says Big.

"Fa' sho'." says Jason. "Now dat I got y'all niggas out my business, let's get some food. I'm drained," grins Jason.

"I'm straight, brah, we gotta be at Mr. Iman's office by 10:30 a.m." says Big.

"Aiight, Imma just meet y'all at the spot then, 'cause I'm hungry as hell," says Jason.

"Cool," says Big. Jason jumps back on the elevator heading down to the garage where his car is parked. Big and Black wait outside for the valet to bring their car back around. The valet parks the car and brings the keys to Black.

"Man, I'm driving," says Big.

"Cool," says Black, he slides the keys across the top of the car.

"Pass through Techwood, I gotta pick up a package," says Black.

"Who you going to see? Dad?" asks Big.

"Hell, yeah, I'm finna scoop da last seven from him right quick. By da time we done there, Jason should already be at the spot," replies Black.

Jason pulled up to the spot about five minutes after Big and Black did. As he sits in the driveway, he thinks to himself that if Mr. Iman could really turn the money they made in the streets into an legitimate business, the next thing he had on his list to do was settle down. Jason

Lynise

was thirty-four; he felt he was getting too old for this life. He was tired of always having to watch his back, tired of the same ol' routine. He wanted a family now. Jason got out of the car and walked toward the house. He turned around to see Ms. Jackson in the window as usual. He threw his hand up to waive at her before he went inside.

"Brah, its 9:00 a.m. in the morning and you on the game," says Jason shaking his head.

"Uh, huh," says Black staring at the T.V.

"Man, y'all cats come on. Y'all know I hate going out der' wit dem stinking ass dogs anyway. I'm trying to get dis shit ova wit so I can get back to da crib," says Big.

"What you rushing for, dat loot ain't gotta be there till, what? After 10:00 a.m.?" says Black still staring at the T.V.

"Dat nigga go brain dead every time he get on dat game, dats why I don't play dem shits, I just got 'em at da crib to entertain y'all ass." says Jason.

"Preciate dat, cuz. Imma be sure to come through more often since you buying us gifts and shit," laughs Black, still not taking his eyes of the game.

"Fuck dat damn game, he ain't coming to the meeting anyway. Mr. Iman gone set aside and account for 'em just in case he have a rainy day out here on these streets.

"That's right," nods Black.

"Come on now, brah, I'm tired as hell. I've been up all night arguing with Monica's ass," says Big. They walk into the kitchen, Big grabs the dog chains and Jason gets the shovel. The dogs start barking and running back and forth in happiness to see their owners.

"Damn, brah, you talk about me…I told you not to marry dat prissy broad, ha we just surprised you still got some money left," laughs Jason

"Ha, ha, ha, my ass nigga…start digging," Big demands. Jason starts to dig a hole in the ground. Big watches him to make sure he was digging in the right spot, he sees a shiny little earring and picks

TWO TIMES BETRAYED

it up.

"Are you digging in the right fucking spot, I don't remember the money being dat deep down," says Big. Jason stops digging to give the shovel to Big when he notices the earring in his hand.

"Lemme see dat, where did you get this?" asks Jason. He studied the earring and almost immediately knew that it was Kila's. He had them custom made for her for her birthday, that was the only pair made. Big saw the expression on Jason's face change as he looked at the earring, out of instinct he fell to the ground and began digging through the shit and mud looking for his money. It wasn't there.

"You got to be fucking kidding me. I know dat fucking bitch ain't took my money!" yells Jason. He gets on his knees to help Big search for their money, hoping they were digging in the wrong spot.

"It ain't fucking here, Jason. What bitch got our fucking money, brah? And please don't say fuckin' Kila, brah!" yells Big. Black comes outside to see Big and Jason covered in mud and dog shit. He can tell by both of the men's faces that he does not want to hear what they have to say.

"Who da fuck's earring is dat?" asks Big.

"What's going on?" asks Black, eating a bag of chips.

"Da money's gone and this muthafucka know who got it," says Big. Black puts the chips down and his hand on his waist for his pistol. He and Jason were friends true enough, but his loyalty was to Big first. "$500,000 fuckin' dollars gone? I want my fucking money, nigga; you better start talking!" yells Big. Jason stands there in disbelief; never in a million years would he have ever thought that that bitch Kila would get him like this.

"It was Kila. I might've fucked up and let some shit slip. I never would've thought dat little bitty bitch would grow balls and do some shit like this," says Jason.

"You mean to tell me, dat hoe, Kila, ridin' around here with my money?" says Black. Jason reaches for his phone to call Kila, it goes straight to voicemail.

Lynise

"Bitch, I can't believe you dat fucking stupid. I want my fucking money hoe, and when I see ya, Imma put a hole in ya…I promise you dat shit, bitch!" yells Jason to Kila's voicemail. Big paces back and forth.

"Imma tell you like this, brah, Imma get my cut whether you gotta sell everything you own, or you can get it just like Imma give to her, I told you not to fuck wit dat trifling as bitch anyway," says Black. Jason attempts to walk toward Black, Big intervenes between the two.

"What da fuck you sayin', brah?" asks Jason.

"You know what da fuck I'm sayin', nigga," replies Black, walking up toward Jason.

"Da bitch got my money too, what da fuck you think I don't want it?" asks Jason.

"Shit nigga, you been so in love lately, how I don't know you and dat bitch ain't plan this shit?" says Black.

"Nigga, fuck you. I ain't plan a muthafuckin' thing; hell is you sayin', brah!" yells Jason.

"I know you no where dat bitch live at brah, we ain't gone get shit standing right here making a scene fa' dat nosey ass lady across the street," says Big.

Jason tries to call Kila again, he doesn't get an answer. Everything that Jason thought he felt for Kila was now gone, he knew he had to find her. He also knew that there was no way she pulled this off by herself. He had to also find Shasta as well.

The three of them got in the car headed straight to Kila's house by Lenox Mall.

"I know where her friend be at too," says Black, referring to Shasta.

"Who?" asks Big.

"Dat other stripper hoe she always with, Shasta," says Black.

The car grew silent. Twenty minutes later, they pulled up in front of Lexington Estates. Kila wasn't home.

Chapter 9

Word had hit the streets quick that Big and his crew were looking for Kila and Shasta. It got so heavy for the girls that Shasta ended up having to take her son out to her aunt's house in Sandy Springs. They were going from hotel to hotel, switching cell phone after cell phone; it started to feel like Atlanta was shrinking.

"We can't keep living like this, if we stay in Atlanta we're dead for sure," says Shasta.

"Damn, you don't think I don't know dat? Where else we gone go? I ain't got no family nowhere else but Atlanta, and I ain't been nowhere else other than Georgia," replies Kila.

"I got a cousin in Miami whose been trying to get me to come down there and work for the longest now," says Shasta.

"Is dat so?" asks Kila sarcastically.

"Is dat so? What da fuck is dat supposed to mean, Kila? It's your fault I'm in this shit now bitch!" yells Shasta.

"My fault? Bitch, you wanted dat money just as bad as I did. Now dat da shit done hit da fan, you wanna blame me like you ain't have your hand in it too, well, fuck you Shasta!" yells Kila back at Shasta.

"Fuck you too bitch! What the hell is you sayin'!" replies Shasta.

"Fuck me? Fuck me? If it wasn't fa' me, yo' ass would still be stuck on Hollywood Road like ya dumb ass sista, Candace, with God knows how many fuckin kids!" yells Kila.

"So, what da fuck you sayin'? You saved me? I don't owe you

Lynise

shit, bitch. My pussy paved da way fa' me to live how I'm living, not yours!" yells Shasta.

"You know what…fuck this shit! I ain't got time fa' this shit. Call your fucking cousin and set it up, but when we get to Miami, you forget we ever fuckin' met!" yells Kila.

"What da fuck you think dats gone be hard fa' me to do? I think fuckin' not, bitch. You already fa' gotten. Matter of fact, get da fuck out my room!" yells Shasta.

"Your room? Aiight. Whatever Shasta, cuz you trippin. Imma dip, but don't get shit twisted, baby girl, 'cause I ain't take dat money by myself. So you go cool off and call me when you get your mind right." Kila grabs her purse and leaves the room. Shasta throws her cup at the door after Kila leaves. Pacing back and forth, she starts to cry asking God why is it so hard to leave this life behind. She feels like every step she takes forward, she has to take ten steps backwards. To her, it seems like no matter how hard she tries to get out the streets, some fucked-up event keeps her tangled in it. Shasta grabs her phone and calls her cousin, Ella.

The phone rings.

"Hello, hello, ah…I got you, leave a message at the beep," says Ella's voicemail.

"I hate when people do dat stupid shit on their phone," says Shasta out loud. She hangs up and calls again. This time Ella answers.

"Hello," says Ella.

"What up lil cuz," says Shasta.

"Shasta? Is dat you?" asks Ella.

"It's me girl, what's good in the sunshine state?" asks Shasta.

Ella gives off one of those screams women do when they ain't seen someone in a while. Shasta pulls the phone away from her ear.

"Calm down girl, what's been up with ya though?" asks Shasta.

"Nothing much cuz, same ol', making as much money as I can, still telling these niggas no while trying to keep these lames off me," laughs Ella.

TWO TIMES BETRAYED

Ella was about two years younger than Shasta, she was Haitian, slim and had everything in the right place. The only thing that would've thrown you off was her eyes, they were naturally green. She stood about 5'7" with real short hair that a man could only wish to caress. Ms. Ella's goodies were only for women. She had never slept with a man in her life. Shasta used to remember back in the day when Ella used to come up for the summer, they would play house and Ella would be somewhere re-inventing the game with girls only. Ella's mother had moved them down to Jacksonville, Florida to so-call "save" Ella from the big city. As soon as Ella turned eighteen, she left home for that big city and Miami is where she has resided every since.

"I was thinking 'bout coming down there to take you up on your offer you been bugging me 'bout, honey," Shasta announces.

"Oh, really, what brings the sudden change of scenery?" asks Ella.

"Does it matter, sweetie?" asks Shasta.

"Not really, Ms. Secretive, so when you plan on coming down?" asks Ella.

"I was thinking 'bout flying out in the morning; me and my home girl Kila, da bitch ain't never been outside Georgia and she wanna come," Shasta elaborates.

"Uh huh, dat's what you said da last time. I ain't gone hold my breath on it, so honey when you get here, call me and I'll have someone come pick y'all up from the airport," says Ella in disbelief of the visit.

"Aiight, then it's a go. We should be there by tomorrow afternoon." says Shasta.

"Uh huh, if you say so, doll," says Ella.

"You'll see, Imma see you tomorrow, love."

"Bye bye, girl," says Ella as they both hang up.

Shasta sits on the edge of the bed thinking of who to call next. It was her son. She dials Aunt Nancy's number.

"Blessed and highly favored, who do you wish to speak to?" asks Aunt Nancy.

Lynise

"It's me Auntie, is Lil' Chris asleep yet?" asks Shasta.

"Nah, baby, let me go get him for you."

"Okay."

"Christopher!" yells Aunt Nancy. "Your mother is on the phone."

A few minutes later Lil' Chris is on the phone with his mom.

"Hey, mommy!" says Lil' Chris excitedly.

"Hi, sweetheart," says Shasta, feeling like everything would be fine, even if that feeling was only temporary.

"When are you coming back to get me?" asks Lil' Chris.

"Soon baby, real soon. Momma just got some things to take care of first, okay sweetie?" says Shasta trying to hold back her tears.

"Are we still getting a new house?" asks Lil' Chris.

"Of course we are; matter of fact, this is what I want you to do for me...ask Auntie Nancy to get you a map, and you pick out any state you want to move to and that's where we are getting our new house at," Shasta tells her son.

"Okay, I will." says Lil' Chris

"I love you, sugar bear," says Shasta.

"I love you too, mommy; always and forever," says Lil' Chris.

"Always and forever...let me talk back to your Auntie, and you go finish getting ready for bed."

"Okay. Auntie Nancy! My mommy wants you!" yells Lil' Chris. He places the phone down on the table and runs back into his room for bed. Aunt Nancy gets the phone.

"Hello," says Auntie Nancy.

"Hey, thank you for taking my son in Auntie. I should be back to get him in a few weeks okay?"

"It's no problem Shasta, me and George enjoy the company since Sherrie and Megan have moved out for college."

"Well, I told Lil' Chris that you were gone get him a map, can you do that for me please?" asks Shasta.

"I will, but are you okay, Shasta?"

"Honestly, no, but I will be soon. I just got a few things I need to clear off my plate and we will be good."

"Give it all up to God, baby. You keep running from Him, all He wants you to do is surrender for He is the only God, and from what I hear, He is the only one that's gone bring you out of whatever you're going through."

"I know Auntie, but I really don't think God's got time to handle or even deal with my problems right now, plus, what I'm going through is the making of my own hands." "God loves you, and He always has time for His children. He's just waiting on you, baby girl."

"Okay, we'll see. Have you talked to my mother?"

"I did earlier, she's worried about you; you need to call her just to let her know you're okay."

"I will, I promise. Next time she calls, be sure to tell her I love her and I'll talk to her when I get situated. I gotta go Auntie, kiss my baby for me and thank you again."

"You're welcome, sweetie," says Auntie Nancy. They both hang up.

Chapter 10

This morning started like any other, excluding the fact that Shasta and Kila were skipping states in order to stay alive. Shasta wanted more than anything to leave Atlanta, but she hates that she had to leave under the current circumstances. Shasta sat up in the middle of the bed to see that Kila had made her way back into her room. As mad as she was at Kila last night, she knew that starting a beef with her was the last thing she needed right now. Shasta felt like she was running out of options. Even when she and Kila made it to Miami, she knew that she couldn't stay down there forever, she had a son to raise. She also knew that just because they temporarily relocated, Big and Jason weren't going to stop looking for them. Shasta didn't want to spend the rest of her life looking over her shoulders. She had to give the money back. Her plan was to go to Miami, get dat money up and make plans to return. Shasta couldn't tell Kila what she planned to do; as close as they were to each other, their relationship over the last few months had started to shift.

Kila wakes up and sees Shasta sitting on the edge of the bed staring out the window.

"Look, I'm sorry I got you into this, but you in it now, and fighting wit me ain't gone keep dem niggas off our back; ain't nothing but one way to get 'em off us, and that's in Miami," Kila says. Shasta turns to look at her; all she can think about is how did she get this way. From dancing to tricking to robbing to not giving a fuck 'bout having a nigga knocked off. All she could do was agree…for now.

"I know," says Shasta.

"I was thinking…you say your cousin, Ella, got something set up fa' whenever you come down, right?" asks Kila.

"Yeah," said Shasta.

"Shit, then we straight; fuck them niggas. Shasta they ain't get dat money legally, they ain't no worse than us, they woulda easily did da same shit to another nigga, trust dat, if he got caught slipping. I say we go down there, make some money, get in the mix, link up wit some niggas that don't give a fuck, and let them solve our problems fa' a nice ticket, like I said," says Kila.

Shasta didn't want to believe what her friend was implying, but she had already went there. The look her friend had in her eyes as she spoke was pure greed; at that point, Shasta realized that her friend would do anything fa' da dollar. This was the beginning of the end for they're friendship and Shasta wasn't fucked up 'bout it, so she just entertained Kila's convo.

"Now you wanna knock 'em off?" asks Shasta sarcastically.

"What you think I wanna be looking over my shoulders forever? Jason gullible ass won't hesitate to knock me off if he gets the opportunity. What's done is done now Shasta, and I'm not gone let them niggas get me before I get them."

Shasta didn't want to admit Kila was right, even though she planned to give the money back, niggas and they pride wasn't gone let it just be over like that. But she figured she would cross that bridge when it came, plus, at the end of the day, she knew how the streets talked and she ain't want three murders hanging over her either. She wanted to end all ties with Kila. If Kila's solution to their problems became official, she would be tied to Kila forever, and at the point she was in in her life, she couldn't mentally or physically take any more friends like Kila; let alone be stuck wit her.

"Aiight, aiight, I don't wanna talk 'bout this shit no more, let's just get there first, and we will go from there."

"Cool, when we leave?" asks Kila.

"Today. Our flight is for 4:00 p.m., when we check out at 11:00 a.m. we're headed straight fa' the airport," says Shasta.

Kila walks toward the bathroom.

"Okay, I gotta make a stop first. Imma meet you back here at 11:00 a.m." says Kila

"Aiight.".

She lays back down in the bed wondering what sort of stop Kila had to make, there were only a hand full of places that Kila hung out, and of those places, it was only a few people that wasn't aware or didn't care about what they had done. Word on the streets was that Big had put a live ticket on them for five racks a piece for whoever finds them. Shasta didn't trust Kila anymore, for that reason alone, she kept her gun close to her. She wanted to quickly end their relationship, and the only way she saw herself making that happen was to give the money back—all without Kila finding out.

Kila comes out the bathroom.

"Don't worry Shasta, everything will be okay, sweetie," Kila says, looking as if she does not have a worry in the world. In her mind, she had money, and wasn't no man gone change that. She grabs her purse off the dresser and leaves the room, headed to Amber's house where she was gone hide the money she stashed from Shasta. They had the rest of the other money divided up on prepaid credit cards.

G STREET CHRONICLES
A LITERARY POWERHOUSE
WWW.GSTREETCHRONICLES.COM

Chapter 11

The girls arrived in Miami around 8:00 p.m., they wanted to get settled in before they met Ella at the club. Shasta gave herself six weeks to get dat money up and be back in Atlanta with her son. Since Miami was the next party city, she knew it wouldn't be long before Kila planted her poison in some random nigga, and she was hoping she would; that meant more time to herself and away from Kila.

"Ooh, look at the pretty palm trees, we gotta hit da beach. I have never been to da beach before, ooh and we gotta go shopping too!" says Kila rambling like an excited kid.

"Slow down girl, damn, you ain't been outside Georgia fa' real huh, honey," laughs Shasta.

"Ha, ha my ass. You ain't been nowhere in a minute either, honey; anyway, what hotel we staying at?" asks Kila.

"Ella booked us a two bedroom suite at da Ritz for a week, it should be a car here too waiting for us."

"This airport is so fucking big, where do we go?" asks Kila.

"This way."

Shasta walks toward baggage claim for their luggage, then out the double doors in the direction of the line of taxis, limos and cars waiting to pick up their guest.

"She says our driver will have a sign with my name on it; look and see if you see it," Shasta says.

"I see 'em."

"Where?" asks Shasta.

"Dat skinny lil white man right there by that black Lincoln in front of the Coca Cola sign," Kila explains. Kila starts walking in direction toward the car, when the girls get to the car, the driver recognizes Shasta as Ella's cousin from a picture Ella had given him. He quickly grabs their bags and introduces himself.

"Good evening, I'm Mr. Henry. I hope your flight was pleasant." The girls just stand there staring at him as he opens the trunk to put their luggage in.

"Ms. Ella wants me to have you ladies at the club by midnight, here's my cell. I will be your driver if needed during the duration of your stay with us," Mr. Henry says.

"I haven't spoken back with Ella yet…what the fuck? She got a GPS in my ass?" laughs Shasta.

"No, ma'am, I don't think she does; however, I am to call her once I drop you both off at the hotel," Mr. Henry says, not cracking a smile.

"Damn, lil cuz, got it like dat?" asks Kila in approval.

Both ladies get in the town car in route to the hotel. Shasta can't help but notice how quiet Kila got once they were in the car. She watches as Kila stares out the window like a little kid waiting anxiously for her turn at the ice cream truck.

"Hey, girl, you alright over there? You mighty quiet," says Shasta.

"Yeah girl, I'm fine. It's just that looking out this window got me bugging. I mean, I ain't never been outside Georgia, and I don't know if it's da trees, or us being chauffeured by Alfre dat got me actually considering changing my life fa' da better; ya know?" Kila says, still staring out the window.

Shasta looks at Kila in shock not believing what she's hearing; she knows that whateva Kila is feeling is only temporary; Kila will never change, and Shasta has finally come to accept it.

"Uh huh, it's the trees, girl," laughs Shasta.

A few minutes later, the ladies pull up at the hotel. Mr. Henry gets their luggage out of the trunk and escorts them inside to the front desk.

"Here are your room keys, I've called Ella to let her know you've checked in already. I'll be back round 11:30 to pick you both up for the club; is there anything else I can do for you before I leave?" asks Mr. Henry.

"No, but thank you for asking, we will be ready at 11:30 p.m." Shasta adds as they get out of the car.

Mr. Henry leaves the ladies in the lobby.

"Come on Shasta, let's go see what this room looks like," says Kila.

"This is a nice hotel, ain't it girl?" asks Shasta.

"Hell, yeah, look at how high these ceilings are," says Kila.

"And look at all these uppity white folks; are they looking at us?" asks Shasta.

Kila looks around to see if they were being stared at.

"I think so, honey."

"Well, let's give them something to look at then," Shasta says with a smile on her face.

She grabs Kila's hand as if she was her man, Kila turns back around and plants a huge wet kiss on Shasta's lips. They could feel the two women at the front desk watching them, so Shasta starts making seductive noises as if they were the only two standing there.

"You think they got da picture, baby cakes?" asks Kila.

"Hell, yeah, muffin," says Shasta. They both walk off in the direction of the elevators, laughing. "So fancy, so fancy," says Kila as she gets on the elevator. They both are tripping so hard they don't even notice the man on the elevator with them.

"What floor?" asks the man. Shasta turns around.

"What the fuck, when you get on here?" asks Shasta. Before he could answer, Kila interrupts.

Lynise

"Oh, you like da man dat be pushing da buttons fa' people just like on T.V.," says Kila.

"Yes, ma'am, I am. What floor would like?" asks the man again.

"Um, 24 I think, our cards say, penthouse 2412." Shasta replies.

"24, it is, ma'am."

"Ooh, bitch, it got to be money down here, you're cousin got us balling like this. I may never go back to Atlanta," says Kila.

"Uh huh, just remember business before pleasure," Shasta replies.

"Believe it."

When they get off the elevator, they enter on to a private floor; at the end of the hall they see PH 2412 and another man standing at the door suited and booted like the butlers you see on T.V. They can see their luggage at the end of the hall as they get closer to the suite. The elevator man walks behind them to introduce them to the guy standing in front of the door.

"This is Mr. Carlton, your personal concierge; anything you need during your stay at the Ritz, he can, and will do for you. Enjoy your stay," the elevator man says with a smile. Kila thanks him and gives him a $20 tip. Mr. Carlton gets their luggage and escorts them into the suite; once inside the suite, Shasta and Kila just stand there in pure amazement. The suite too has gorgeous high ceilings and the floors are marbled with gold speckled designs in them. The suite has a full bar in it and the living room area has was a flat screen T.V. mounted on the wall. Each room has its own bathroom, with walk-in closets that look like separate apartments. On their beds are white roses and a gift basket from Ella filled with fruits, chocolates, some loud and a bottle of Roseau. All the walls are filled with expensive pictures and last, but not least, they have a view of the beach to die for. It is a temporary heaven for them.

"Damn, girl, outta all the hotels we done stayed in, I ain't never been in one as fly as this one," says Kila.

"Girl, me either, you gotta be getting to da money to cop something like this, Lil' Ella said it be bumping down here; but I would've never guessed it was jumping off like this."

"Man, baby cakes, I got a vision…fucking around down here we can get some real fucking money; fuck some thousand…I want dat million-dollar status, and I promise you Imma get it," Kila insists.

"I figadilya," says Shasta as she keeps in mind that she, too, has her own vision; and it was nowhere near what Kila has planned. Shasta wants to get in and out.

"Let's gone and get ready before Alfre comes back for us," Kila says.

"Before I do anything, I gotta put me one in the air, and while I'm at it, pop dat bottle of Roseau," Shasta replies.

"Where da hell you get some green from dat fast?" asks Kila.

"My pussy," replies Shasta.

"Ewwww...smoke on then, chic," Kila laughs.

"I'm just playing, you ain't check your gift basket I take it," says Shasta.

"Hell, naw, bitch; I didn't. Since when did they start putting marijuana in fruit baskets?' asks Kila.

"When da fruit baskets come from my cousin Ella, it even got blunts in them," Shasta confirms.

"Oh, yeah, that's what I'm talking 'bout! We should've been made this move."

A couple hours later, they are both buzzed, dressed and calling Mr. Henry to chauffeur them to club to meet up with Ella.

G STREET CHRONICLES
A LITERARY POWERHOUSE
WWW.GSTREETCHRONICLES.COM

Chapter 12

The black Lincoln town car pulls up to the club at exactly 12:00 a.m. on the dot. Not only was Mr. Henry proper, he was on time. There was a long line of people waiting to get inside the club, and an even longer VIP line; people were also casually posted up in the parking lot politican. Mr. Henry escorts the ladies to the front of the VIP line. They hear a couple of haters complaining about them jumping the line; however, Shasta and Kila are feeling themselves so much, they simply tooted their nose and ignored them.

"Well, well, well, Mr. Henry were did you find these beautiful ladies at?" asks the doorman who is lustily staring at Shasta and Kila.

"They're Ella's family from Atlanta," Mr. Henry says as he introduces the ladies. Shasta and Kila have all eyes on them; people can't help but noticed how the doorman is drooling all over them. Shasta is dressed in a gold, fitted miniskirt dress, she has her hair beveled flat, and a pair of black stilettos on. Kila was decked out in a red, two-piece short outfit that grabs attention to her breast, and a pair of high strap heels that show off her legs.

"My name is Smokey, and any friend of Ella's is a friend of mine," the doorman says. He lifts the rope and allows the ladies and Mr. Henry into the club. Immediately, they are greeted by Ella.

"Ah!" screams Ella. "I see y'all made it."

They all issued out hugs.

"How's the room? Do you like it?" asks Ella.

Lynise

"Hell, yeah!" says Kila.

"I gotta say Lil' Cuz, you got down with it," Shasta adds.

"Dats what's up. I knew y'all would like it, come on...my table is over there," Ella points toward the corner.

The club is for sure baller-riffic as well. Ella has her own section in the VIP area, and they could look down from her booth and see everyone in the club. Ella signals the waitress over to them.

"Get me a bottle of Roseau' sugar, and tell da DJ to put on some Young Jeezy; we got Atlanta in da house," says Ella excitedly. A few minutes later, the waitress brings their champagne and Young Jeezy's Bottom of the Map begins beating through the speakers. The DJ also gives Shasta and Kila a shout out, welcoming them to the city.

"Now, this is the life," Kila says as she begins to relax. They all toast.

"To bigger and better things," Shasta offers.

"You better believe it!" Kila adds.

"Tonight, we party, my sweets; tomorrow we get down to business," Ella adds.

"I wouldn't see it no other way," replies Shasta.

The way the VIP section is setup, they had their own private area with tall, mirrored doors you could see out off but not in. It also has its own full service bar and waitress. The table has a built-in fish tank filled with the most beautiful fish you could ever imagine. Off to the right of the VIP room, there was an open shower with a swing set hanging from the top. To the left was a waterfall that flowed to bottom of the club. Shasta and Kila sat back on the couch and soaked in the view. Ella signaled for Mr. Henry.

"Yes, ma'am," Mr. Henry replies.

"Go tell Smokey I need my medicine," says Ella.

"Will do."

A short second later, Smokey comes through the door.

"You gone love this, Ms. Ella; this came straight off the boat," Smokey says. He pulls a small sandwich bag out his pocket and pours the contents on a plate Ella has on the table, she uses her pinky nail to dip up the coke.

"Ooh, ooh, is this that Peru?" says Ella, sucking her teeth.

"And you know it, I told you it was fresh off the boat," Smokey laughs.

"You want some?" asks Ella, looking at Shasta and Kila.

"Naw, I'm good," says Shasta while she takes another sip of her champagne.

"Fuck it, I will," Kila says with a smile. She grabs the rolled up one hundred dollar bill from Ella and snorts the cocaine like a pro.

"Now that's what I'm talking 'bout lil' mama," Smokey adds with a smile. "You let me know if you need anything else, Ms. Ella; and you, you come holler at me before y'all dip. I got somebody I want you to meet," Smokey says looking at Kila. Kila nods back at Smokey in approval of the meeting as he walks off.

"Uh huh, look at you, Miss thang, you ain't been here a day yet and you already got one of owners sending fa' ya," Ella comments.

"Ain't nothing wrong with sayin' hey; ain't dat right Shasta?" asks Kila.

"Sure ain't, baby cakes, who is the other jackpot? Hell, I wanna tell his ass hey too," laughs Shasta.

"You crazy as hell girl, but your he is a her honey, matter of fact, that her is Kila's he's wife. They own this spot and about three or four other spots between here and Daytona; so calling them a jackpot is an understatement, dem muthafuckas is da bank! Don't worry my Shasta, she like girls too," laughs Ella.

"Damn, I think I'm right for both of them then," laughs Kila. They all laughed out loud. Kila bends down for another line, and Ella follows behind. Line after line, after line. They get so high off that blow they don't even notice that Shasta has thrown back a bean and is stripped down to her panties, swinging back and forth in the shower on the swing set. Ella slaps the cute Latin girl on the ass who is dancing in front of her, and points her toward Shasta's direction.

Lynise

"Go show my cousin a good time," says Ella.

"Be sure to take everything off too," replies Kila. The girl looks back and winks her eye in agreement to them.

The girls enjoyed the night away, if it wasn't for Mr. Henry…who knows where they would've woke up at.

Chapter 13

Knock. Knock.
"Housekeeping," the voice of the maid comes through the door. Both Kila and Shasta are still passed out asleep on the sofa and can't hear the maid address herself as she enters the penthouse.

"Excuse me, housekeeping. I brought fresh towels and linen," announces the maid. The housekeeper walks into the living room where the ladies were lying, she opens the large curtains and begins to straighten up; she had just worked a double shift and this was next to the last suite on her list before heading home. Shasta awakes first to see the maid cleaning off the bar; she rubs her eyes, stretches, then reaches for the half of blunt that is in the astray.

"What time is it?" asks Shasta to the maid.

"It's 2:00 p.m. ma'am," the maid replies.

"Damn, really? I'm tired as hell and I got a major fucking headache," Shasta says. The maid walks in to the first bathroom and comes out with a glass of water and aspirin.

"According to Mr. Henry, you ladies partied mighty hard last night," the maid grins as she hands Shasta the water and aspirin.

"Ha, ha, we sure did, the last thing I remember is dancing in the shower with some Puerto Rican girl," laughs Shasta.

"Ah, yes, I remember those days, my sweet. Young, vibrant, and full of energy. Y'all two put me in the mind of me and a good friend of mine from back in the day when I used to cut a rug and hang out

Lynise

all night. My…my…my, how times have passed," the maid says in a moment of reflection. Shasta gets up and goes to the bathroom to get herself together; minutes later, she hears the sound of Kila's voice talking to the maid.

"Where's the menu for room service?" asks Kila.

"In the kitchen, I'll get it for you" the maid replies.

"Thanks, my stomach feels like I haven't eaten in days."

"Alcohol does that to you, sweetie." says the maid.

"Tell me about it," replies Kila.

"Well, sugar, my work here is done, time for me to go grace the next suite with my presence. The number for room service is at the bottom of the menu; call me if you need anything else," states the maid.

"Thank you Mrs…" says Kila.

"Mrs. Carter…and you are very welcome, be sure to see after your friend just like you, she wasn't feeling so good."

"I will." says Kila as she closes the door behind her.

"Look who finally got they ass up," said Shasta.

"Whateva, honey, I been up for a minute now, sitting here politican wit Mrs. Carter." replied Kila.

"Mrs. Carter? Who is dat?" asks Shasta.

"You know, the housekeeping lady," replies Kila.

"Oh, oh yeah, she was nice wasn't she?"

"Yeah, she was. She reminds me of Big Chris' momma, dat lady was too nice, she used to creep me out every time I went with you to drop Lil' Chris off."

"Ugh, there you go spoiling a good conversation, dat bastard was nowhere near on my mind!" Shasta says in disgust.

"My bad girl, I'm 'bout to go get in the shower anyway, so by the time I get out, it should be off your mind and that frown you rocking should be a smile," Kila tries to get Shasta out of the, "I hate my baby daddy mode."

"Ha ha, ha, ain't nothing Kush can't cure," she replies.

"Oh, yeah, I ordered room service for us too so listen out fa' da door."

"What you order?" asks Shasta.

"Shit…every damn thang. Steak, eggs, coffee, orange juice, bagels, muffins, and another bottle of Roseau'." Kila smiles.

"Shit girl, you sure all you and Mrs. Carter do was talk, all dat food, I'm da one wit da fuckin munches," laughs Shasta.

"I'm a big girl in my mind, honey; I gotta eat," laughs Kila.

Shasta sits back on the sofa and puts another blunt in the air as Kila disappears into the bathroom to shower. A few minutes later, room service is at the door with their order. Shasta collects the food, gives the man a $50 bill and closes the door behind him.

"The food's here!" yells Shasta.

"Okay, I'm getting out now," yells Kila.

Shasta sets the table for both of them to eat.

"Damn, dats a big ass steak, what the fuck did they kill da cow downstairs?" laughs Kila.

"It is a big ass steak ain't it?" laughs Shasta.

"Pass me dat bottle of Roseau', my orange juice tastes weird" Kila frowns.

"Your and alchi—it's 3:00 p.m. and you're already getting started, lady," says Shasta.

"And? Just call it pre-happy hour, shit…it's nite nite time in China, so I'm justified. What? You don't want none?" asks Kila.

"Of course I do, I hate juice," says Shasta. They both laugh as they toast their glasses together.

"Anyway, muffin, it's down to business today. Mr. Henry gone be here to pick us up round five; he gone take us shopping for tonight. Then we gotta meet Ella at the club around nine so she can introduce us to the owner, Mac."

"Who da hell is Mac?" asks Kila.

"The nigga who owns da club Ella works at," replies Shasta.

"Oh, yeah, dats what's up."

"Speaking of club owners, did you ever meet dat nigga Smokey

Lynise

was talking 'bout?"

"Hell yeah, girl, while you was swinging in the shower he came up. Baby cakes, dat nigga black as hell; his name should've been fucking Smokey," laughs Kila.

"So what da move is, you gone fuck wit em?" asks Shasta.

"Sure is, his money go way long, I may spaz out every now and then, but I ain't stupid. He say call 'em when we get set up and he gone take me out. I got his number, but Imma wait a minute before I ring his line."

"Dat's right ma-ma, make dat nigga wait on it."

"Believe it."

They both high five each other.

"Damn. I'm full now, come on, let's get dressed; you know Mr. Henry is one on time muthafucka."

"Hell yeah, he is, ain't he girl?" laughs Kila.

The ladies parted to their rooms to get dressed; minutes later, they were in front of the hotel watching as Mr. Henry pulled up.

Chapter 14

Meanwhile back in Atlanta, Big, Jason, and Black were still on the hunt for Shasta and Kila. It had been close to three weeks now, and it seemed they both had disappeared off the face of the planet. Jason was still going to Loops just to see what he could find out. He couldn't get word on Kila's whereabouts, but he did find out where Shasta's baby daddy lived. Big Chris had a lil condo on the eastside, the irony of it, is that he got the info from Amber. Little did he know that if he had reached out to her three weeks ago, he would've been closer to his money because she still had a number for Kila then. Amber was not a friend to Kila or Shasta, she was known in the club for being a stupid, trailer-trash ass hoe who would do any and everything for the dollar; and just as sure as shit stunk, she would've told Jason where they were. Kila knew what type of female Amber was, hell she had some of her same traits. Unbeknownst to her, however, Amber was so spaced out that Kila had hid the money at her house and she ain't even have a clue it was there. Jason called Big to inform him on the new lead he had just gotten from Amber.

Big's phone rings.

"Yo', I got an address to dat bitch Shasta's baby daddy, I'm pretty sure dat nigga knows something," said Jason.

"Oh yeah, where you at now?" asked Big.

"At da barber shop on Bankhead and Hollywood Road," Jason replied.

Lynise

"Aiight, stay put. Me and Black will be there in 15."

"Aiight." Jason replies. They both hang up, fifteen minutes later, Big and Black pulled up. Jason gets in the car, due to the major loss they all had just taken, there was no usual dap downs, there was only tension between them and it was obvious that it was not gone change until that check resurfaced.

"Yo', where we going?" asked Big.

"On Panola, he gotta spot right off the exit next to the Wal-Mart." replied Jason

"Talking 'bout them condos across from Pine Wood?" asked Black.

"Yeah," replied Jason

"Oh okay, I know exactly where we going, I used to fuck with a bitch over there," says Black.

Twenty minutes later, they pull up in front of Big Chris's house. They park across the street; the bitch, Amber told Jason that Big Chris drove and all white Denali. The three of them park outside for almost four hours before Big Chris pulls up. Sad to say that anytime they parked in Alpharetta for four hours in front of someone's house, the police would've been called. They watched Big Chris go in the house, he was alone. Black went around to the back, Big and Jason stayed out front. Shasta's baby daddy was not a street nigga, even though he grew up in the projects; he was book smart and always thought that he was better than the street niggas he grew up around. Jason knocks on the door.

"Who is it?" asked Big Chris.

"Jehovah's Witness, sir" said Jason. Big Chris opened the door with the chain still latched in an attempt to tell them whatever came to mind first; but before he could say anything, Big kicked the door in, and while he was doing so, Black was kicking in the back door.

"Where da fuck Shasta and dat bitch Kila at!" yelled Big. Big Chris holds his nose because the door caught him in the face and immediately his nose began to bleed.

"Where who? Shasta? I don't fucking know! I don't fuck with her anymore man; I gotta wife!" replied Big Chris. Black walks up

TWO TIMES BETRAYED

behind him and puts the 44 caliber to his head.

"Nigga we gone ask you one more time, and you betta think real hard on yo' answer," Black says in a manner that says he means business. Jason grabs Big Chris and throws him on the couch.

"Yo' baby momma and her trifling ass friend Kila took 500 racks from me, and a lil birdie told me dat you know where they hiding at." said Jason. Black still has the pistol pointed at him.

"Man, man…I swear to you, I don't fuck wit her, I'm going to court right now trying to get custody of my son from her; all I know is where her sister Candace lives, I swear man. I don't know nothing," said Big Chris hysterically. Black hits him over the head with the pistol.

"Aaaaah!" screams Big Chris.

"Fuck dat shit you talking cuz, you know something. I know you done heard in the streets what's up," says Big.

"Man, I swear to you, I don't know where she is. Look in the drawer right there and you will see da court papers. I promise cuz, I don't fuck wit da bitch," said Big Chris hoping that the papers would convince them of his innocence. Black goes to the kitchen for the court papers.

"He's telling da truth, but I still don't trust this muthafucka, he still may be leaving something out," said Black.

"Aiight, my nigga, last time…where in da fuck is Shasta?" asks Jason.

Black cocks the 44 back and puts it to Big Chris' head this time.

"Hold on, hold on man, she got an Aunt in Sandy Springs. 5476 Poster Lane, please don't hurt my son, I don't know nothing about nothing, please don't hurt my son," begs Big Chris with tears coming down his face now.

"It's too late fa' dat now," said Big. Big backs up from Big Chris and Black shoots him in the back of the head—execution style.

"Damn, my nigga, what the fuck you do that for?" asks Jason.

"You been playing captain saver long enough, what you want the nigga to warn them we coming. I'm just tying up loose ends," replied

Lynise

Black.

"Come on let's go, fuck dat nigga now, he at peace," said Big.

Jason wipes his fingerprints from off the door, and races to the car following behind Big and Black.

"What was that address again?" asked Big.

"5476 Poster Lane," said Black.

"Aiight, aiight, so what da plan is?" asks Jason.

"Nigga, what you mean, 'what da plan is'? We go over there and make dat bitch tell us where her niece is, dats what the fucking plan is!" replied Black. He reaches in the back to grab another shirt to change into.

"Fuck nigga, we ain't going to fucking Bankhead. This bitch lives in fucking Alpharetta, its three black niggas grilled out wit dreads driving around in the suburbs looking fa' a house ain't none of us been to. How fast do you think it's gone take them uppity ass folks to call 12?" asks Jason.

"Yeah, you right," said Big.

"If he so right, then how the hell we supposed to get what we need?" asks Black.

"Let's just get up there first, check out the scene and we go from there," replied Jason.

Thirty minutes later, they were parked outside Aunt Nancy's house. It had to be pure luck because her neighbors across the street were having a party and from the looks of the guest, they were black folk, so they blended in well with the crowd. Aunt Nancy even had her garage door open, and from where they were parked, you couldn't tell if someone was there or not.

"Da way dat party jumping off, we can sit back for a sec, then when a few more cars fill up this cul-de-sac, Jason can go knock on the door and ask the bitch for some ice or something," said Black.

"Dats probably da smartest shit you done said all night," replied Jason.

"Pssf, whateva nigga," said Black. The cul-de-sac starts to fill with cars as the men sit back and wait for the perfect opportunity.

Chapter 15

Mr. Henry arrives at Mac's club the same time Ella pulls up. Ella drove a cocaine white Range Rover on some 24's; the music is blasting so loud and she is vibing so hard, she ain't even notice Shasta tapping on her window till she turned the truck off.

"You jamming mighty hard, lil' cuz," said Shasta.

"Sure is, doll; I gotta bang Weezy in order to get my head on straight before a prosperous night at work," laughs Ella. Kila walked over to them after saying goodbye to Mr. Henry.

"Hi, sweetness," said Kila as she hugged Ella.

"Halo, turn around and let me look at you," says Ella. Kila spins around for Ella to observe what she is wearing.

"Uh, huh, you both look like money. Mac will be pleased," says Ella. They all walk into the club. Ella makes her way to the bar with Shasta and Kila following behind.

"Aye, Monk-E, give me three shots of Conjours please," Ella places her order.

"Um Ella, I hope he don't put nothing in my damn drink," says Shasta.

"Why you say dat?" asks Ella.

"Cuz you just called the bartender a fucking monkey," replies Kila.

"Girl, dats his name. I was bugging when I first heard it too. It will grow on you, just say it right or his punk ass will get mad," Ella laughs.

Ella grabs Kila by the arm and the three of them disappear into the back office to meet Mac. Mac is tall, dark and slim; you would've thought that he and Kevin Garnett were twins if it wasn't for the mouth full of platinum teeth, Jamaican accent and dreads down his back that are so long he has to keep then tied up so they don't drag on the floor. His Jamaican ascent is deep to no understanding, since he lived in Miami since early childhood, and he rarely visited Kingston. It was for sure a mystery to Ella on why his English was so blank. Erotic Blaze was one of many strip clubs he owned on the east coast, he and Ella were good friends and since she was eighteen, he had always looked out for her. Mac walked in the room to see Ella sitting in his chair.

"Wot mi tel ya 'bout mi chair, little gurl."

"Dere goes da mon of the hour," Ella says, imitating Mac's Jamaican accent. Ella gets up to give him a hug.

"Wen nar you gon grow, mi ladi," said Mac as he hugs her back.

"Ha ha, ha, Mac these are the girls from Atlanta I was telling you about."

Mac turns around to face them.

"Um ok, stand up an lemme si you," Mac says. Shasta and Kila get up from the couch for Mac to observe them.

"So far, so good; nah lemme mi si y'all wit ya clothes off," said Mac. The ladies did as told and stripped down to the nude, Mac circles them to get a full look of their bodies. He cuts his eyes at Ella in satisfaction of what he is viewing.

"Good job, Ms. Ella."

"My pleasure," she replies.

"So when we start?" asks Kila.

"Tonight, if you want," Mac replies.

"Then tonight it is," says Shasta.

"Okay, mi luv, get out mi office. I got sum wok to do, I'm leaving fa' New York in ah couple hours, so mi need you to make sure mi club runs smooth while mi gone," said Mac.

"Don't I always, babe?" asks Ella. Mac winks his eye at Ella, and they all leave him in peace alone with his body guard.

"Did y'all buy something to wear wit Mr. Henry?" asks Ella.

"Not really, but I can make it work for tonight," replied Shasta.

"Don't worry, I saw Ms. Mary Benz out front, she got everything you need in the dressing room, follow me," said Ella. The ladies follow Ella back to the front of the club, which wasn't that big. It was a wide open space with two stages; all the walls are mirrored and the bar is set off to the right of the club by the entrance. There is only one VIP room, so the girls had to bid for time to use it. Mainly, only the girls Ella liked were able to bid time. The rest of them had to settle for working the floor.

"Every time you leave and come back, you bring more girls wit you, I see why you're Mac's favorite pet," grinned Ms. Mary.

"Now...now, be nice Ms. Mary, this is my cousin Shasta and her friend Kila. They need something to wear," said Ella. They all exchanged greetings then Ms. Mary took them to the dressing rack.

"Gone now, honey, they will be fine, Imma send 'em up once they dressed," said Ms. Mary.

"Okay, honey," replied Ella and she left the ladies to attend the club.

"Now, who's first?" asks Ms. Mary. Kila walks toward her first anxiously wanting to see what she had.

"You look like a size seven," Ms. Mary says to Kila.

"And you a size five," she says to Shasta. She starts giving the ladies clothes to cipher through.

"All my outfits come with matching garter belts and heels, prices start at $75, but since you're Ella's people, you can have 'em for $50 a piece," said Ms. Mary. Shasta and Kila found five outfit's a piece, while Kila was changing Shasta paid Ms. Mary for both of their clothes, then she changed as well.

"How do we look?" asked Shasta.

Lynise

"Like some high-class, top notch hoes," replied Ms. Mary smiling.

"Dats da look we were going for," laughs Kila.

"I think I may like you young lady," said Ms. Mary.

"Same hear," says Kila. As trifling as Kila was, it was easier for her to befriend people than it was for Shasta. Ms. Mary had one of the other girls take them to the front were Ella was.

"Ooh, ooh, now y'all are too fine to be working here," Ella says as she admires the see-through black and white outfits they are rocking.

"Why haven't you changed?" asks Shasta.

"I'm not working tonight, I only work on nights Mac here all night. I gotta watch the spot, but don't worry, Imma be around; y'all go do y'all thing and show these shones what da "A" hit like," said Ella.

Shasta and Kila left Ella at the bar and disappeared into the crowd.

Chapter 16

"A'ight, show time," said Big. Jason gets out the car and walks across the street to Shasta's aunt's house. He rings the doorbell; a few seconds later Aunt Nancy opens the door.

"Yes, can I help you?" asked Aunt Nancy.

"Yes, ma'am, um…as you can see we're having a party across the street, and I was wondering if I could have some ice. I would go to the store, but my car is blocked in and I really need some ice for the margaritas," said Jason.

"I usually don't let strange men in my house, but you look okay," replied Aunt Nancy.

"Thank you, thank you. You're a life saver," said Jason. He thought to himself she would've never let Black or Big in her house; he has the clean-cut look of the three; minus the dreads. He follows her to the kitchen. Big stays in the car while Black stands in the garage waiting for Jason to call his phone.

"You have a beautiful home, you would've never guessed it was this big from the outside," said Jason.

"Thank you, here's your ice, son. How long do you think all that hoopla gone continue over there?" asks Aunt Nancy.

"Um, I don't know Miss…" said Jason as he presses buttons on his phone.

"My name is Ms. Nancy and yours?" asks Aunt Nancy.

"Ja- Jake," replied Jason. The hesitation in Jason's voice when

Lynise

he gave his name made her feel uncomfortable, as she attempts to quickly get him out her house, Black kicks in her garage door. Aunt Nancy tries to run, but Jason grabs her and puts his hands over her mouth before she can scream. Black was across from them with his gun cocked back.

"We ain't come here to hurt you, just tell us where your niece is and we will be on our way," Jason says.

Aunt Nancy starts to cry.

"I- I- I don't know where she is," she hysterically says.

"Look bitch, I ain't got time fa' this shit. Where da fuck is ya niece at?" asks Black as he hits Aunt Nancy across the face with the pistol.

"Come on lady, I can only hold him off fa' so long," said Jason.

"Imma ask you one more time, where is she?" yells Black. Aunt Nancy keeps quiet. Jason notices Aunt Nancy staring at the phone on the counter. He went to pick it up and scrolled through the caller ID. Shasta Smithson was the last call she got, with a 305 area code. He calls the number. It goes straight to voicemail and he stores the number in his phone.

"So they in Miami, huh?" asks Jason. Aunt Nancy remains quiet.

"Its okay, your silence confirms my question" said Jason.

"You got what you want, do what you gone do and get the fuck out my house!" yells Aunt Nancy.

"Ah, look who's getting feisty. I gotta give it to ya, you got more heart than that sucka ass baby daddy of hers" said Black as he rubs the gun across her face.

"Come on, let's go, we got what we came for; this bitch ain't finna tell us nothing," said Jason.

"I can make her," said Black staring at Aunt Nancy with a demented look on his face.

"Naw, nigga, let's bounce," said Jason.

"You've been spared this time, but be sure if this info don't lead nowhere, you will see me again, and so will her bastard ass son," replied Black. Jason instructs Aunt Nancy to the ground, face down.

TWO TIMES BETRAYED

"Oh yeah, and if you call the police, her son is dead. I know where he goes to school." said Black.

"Thanks for the ice," said Jason. They both exit out the garage. Big has the car running and they speed off.

"Where are dey?" asks Big.

"Miami," replies Jason.

"Fo' sho'?" said Big.

"Yes, sir!" said Black.

"Cool, to Miami we go; let's go get my fuckin' money and show dem hoes who dey fucking stole from," said Big.

Aunt Nancy watched out the window as they pulled off—crying hysterically. She grabs the phone to call her husband, George and she also began calling Shasta repeatedly, but she didn't get an answer.

"Got damn it girl, what have you gotten yourself into? Two men wit guns just left my house looking for you. You need to call me, ASAP!" yells Aunt Nancy to Shasta's voicemail. Aunt Nancy then sat on the kitchen floor and waited for her husband to come home.

G STREET CHRONICLES
A LITERARY POWERHOUSE
WWW.GSTREETCHRONICLES.COM

Chapter 17

Shasta and Kila didn't go back to the room after the club, instead they spent the night over Ella's. Ella had a huge three bedroom condo right on the strip. Mac brought it for her on her twenty-first birthday as a present; it had a similar design as the suite they were staying in at the hotel. When Shasta woke up, she grabbed her phone, wanting to hear the sound of her son's voice; she and Kila had been in Miami for 'bout a week now, and on the run from Big for 'bout a month. She missed her son and almost had enough money to return to Atlanta. Before she could dial Aunt Nancy's number, she notices she has thirty-six missed calls from her. Her heart drops and she begins to feel sick thinking the worst. Shasta nervously dials her aunt's number. Her uncle picks up on the first ring.

"Why haven't you been answering your phone? We've been calling you all fucking night?" Uncle George says angrily.

"My ringer was off, I had to work. Why? What's wrong? Is Lil' Chris okay?" asks Shasta, rambling. She looks up to see Ella and Kila coming through the front door with breakfast. Kila notices the look on Shasta's face and knew something was wrong.

"Yes, Lil' Chris is fine, as far as your aunt, she was beat in the face with a pistol by two men that came by looking for you!" said Uncle George. Shasta drops to the ground and tears begin to run from her face. Kila knew something was up now.

"I'm so sorry; how is she? Is she okay?" asks Shasta.

Lynise

"She's fine, she's more worried for you though, baby girl; what have you gotten yourself into this time?" asks Uncle George.

"I dunno, Unc, I dunno; did Lil' Chris see anything?" asks Shasta.

"No, he slept through the whole thing" replied Uncle George.

"I need to speak to him," said Shasta.

"I don't think that's a good idea right now, I want you to calm down and don't worry about us. I got the guys over, and we will be ready if them punks decide they wanna come back. You just do whatever you gotta do to see that your problems go away," said Uncle George.

"Okay, tell my aunt I'm so sorry and I never intended for any of this to happen" Shasta said with tears still running down her face.

"She knows sweetie, remember what I said, we will talk soon; we love you and take care of yourself," said Uncle George.

"I love y'all too," replied Shasta. They both hung up. Shasta broke down and began to cry even harder.

"What's wrong? What happened?" asked Kila nervously.

"Are you okay, cuz? What's going on?" asks Ella.

"They know where we are," said Shasta. Kila sat down next to Shasta, Ella stood in front of them.

"They who, what da fucks up cuz?" asked Ella.

"Are you sure?" asked Kila.

"Yes, I'm sure! My aunt has the bruises to prove it!" yells Shasta.

"What's going on Shasta? What happen to Auntie Nancy?" demands Ella.

"We got into some trouble back in Atlanta," said Kila.

"Um okay, what kinda of trouble?" asks Ella. Shasta checked her voicemail, and there was a message from Jason, after listening to it her eyes turned to Kila. Kila notices her whole facial expression changed from fear to pure anger. Shasta gets off the floor and walks toward the kitchen where Ella's bar is. She pours herself a drink and makes them one as well.

"Aye, baby cakes, how much money was in them dog pins?" asks Shasta as she turns her cup up to finish her drink in one swallow.

TWO TIMES BETRAYED

"What you mean? $122k. You was there when we counted it," replied Kila. Ella moved away from her cousin, even though they didn't grow up around each other, she could tell from the look on her face when she asked her question that if it wasn't the right answer, she was about to do something to Kila, and she didn't want to be in the way.

"Umm, dat's funny cause I just got a message from Jason saying dat him Big and Black are on their way to Miami and dey want the 500 fucking racks!" yells Shasta. Kila's jaw drops, her look confirms that Jason wasn't lying.

"I'm sorry Shasta, I didn't mean to get anyone hurt, I didn't think they…" said Kila. Shasta ran up to Kila and before she could finish her sentence, Shasta punches her in the face. Shasta hit Kila in the face repeatedly, blackening both her eyes and busting her lip; she was beating Kila so bad that Ella had to shoot in the air to get her off her.

"Now dat y'all done. What da fuck y'all gone do, cause it's obvious dat y'all can't keep running," said Ella. Breathing heavily, Shasta walks back over to Kila and helps her off the ground.

"We in this till the end, I'm not gone let them hurt me, promise you dat!" said Shasta still catching her breath.

"Ya know Nicko live down here now, here is his number. If you need 'em call 'em, you fam and we ain't finna let them niggas fuck with you," said Ella excluding Kila from the conversation.

"Miami is a big city, we gotta find out where they at first," said Kila.

"Mr. Henry can do dat for us, he's ex military and still got some connections, Imma call 'em now. Y'all go clean yourself up, and Kila, honey, you gone need some makeup,"

"I just wanna know where da fuck is da rest of the money at?" asks Shasta.

"Over Amber's house" said Kila as she held a bag of ice over her lip.

"You mean to tell me you left over 300 racks over fucking

Lynise

Amber's house? Kila, what da fuck is wrong wit you? I should hit yo' ass again," said Shasta, still mad as hell. Kila just stood there staring at her, she knew she deserved all that Shasta was issuing out because she knew that if the tables were reversed, it would be Shasta wit a busted lip.

"Yes. She will never find it though, we both know how dumb Amber is. I hid it in the walls of her attic," replied Kila.

"That's just great, we got niggas trying to kill us fa' money we ain't even fucking got and to make matters worse, your trifling ass just had to be greedy. We been friends for seven years and I would've done anything for you. How could you cross me like this, never in a million years would I have done something like this to you, Kila," said Shasta angrily. Shasta was not only mad, she was hurt.

"Muffin, I'm sorry. Please, please fa' give me; as soon as we get back to Atlanta, the money is yours," said Kila. Shasta sits in disbelief. She knows that from the message Jason left on her voicemail, wasn't no negotiating; she knows what she has to do and she has no time to waste doing it.

"Uh, huh Kila, whateva, just leave me alone for a minute. I gotta get my thoughts together."

A few hours pass. Ella comes out her room, she had left them alone to vent.

"I just got off the phone wit Mr. Henry, he says three men fitting da description of Jason and them just checked into da Hilton across da street from y'all hotel. He took pictures of them fa' me, he's on his way now to show us," said Ella.

"Thanks cuz, I wonder if they know we're staying right across from them, if that's them," said Shasta. Shasta knew Jason was the brains of the three and he was good with computers too.

"I don't think so, but considering how fast they got down here, if that's them, it's only a matter of time before they find out," said Ella.

Kila sat on the couch, quiet as ever.

"Shit, I can't believe they found us dat fast. I mean, how? I heard

TWO TIMES BETRAYED

Jason was a computer geek, but damn," Shasta says in disbelief.

"I dunno cuz, it could be a number of things. Shit…starting with yo' phone, did you call anyone from your phone or da room?" asked Ella.

"No, I just called Auntie Nancy to check on Lil' Chris," said Shasta. She thought of what she had just said.

"Damn it! I transferred my service to a Florida number soon as we got off the plane. They must've gotten my number from Auntie Nancy's caller ID. Shit…shit…shit!" said Shasta. She reaches in her pocket and pulls out the phone, shaking her head.

"Lemme see it," asks Ella. Shasta gives Ella the phone and Ella throws it on the ground and stomps it with her six-inch Jimmy Chew stilettos. She knew with the usage of a little technology, they could easily track Shasta's and Kila's whereabouts with a little internet help.

"Call your voicemail and get da number he called from, we might need it lata," stated Ella.

"Okay." Shasta walks over toward Kila and grabs her phone too. She stomps hers as well.

"Why you break my phone? I ain't call nobody," said Kila.

"I ain't taking no more chances on you, honey." Shasta stares Kila dead in the face. Shasta did not trust her at all; if she was capable of something like this, she ain't want to risk putting nothing past her. A few minutes later, Mr. Henry was at the door. Ella directs him to the living room where Shasta and Kila are. Mr. Henry takes out a folder that had the pictures of the men in it and places them on the table.

"Is everything okay, Ms. Ella?" asks Mr. Henry in concern.

"Yes, everything is fine, hang around for awhile. There's food in the kitchen, make yourself at home. I need to speak to them privately please."

Mr. Henry nods his head and then leaves for the kitchen. Kila picks up the folder and looks at the pictures Mr. Henry has taken.

"Is it them?" asks Ella.

"Yes," replied Kila as she starts to rock back and forth in the chair.

Lynise

She had a bad feeling, and for the first time in her life, she didn't know what to do. Kila started to examine her life, and began to regret most of the decisions she had made that got her to where she was now. Fucked up. Ella got on the phone and called Nicko. Shasta went to the bar and poured them all another drink, this time she used bigger cups.

Chapter 18

"Did you get in touch wit Mr. Iman?" asked Jason.
"Yeah," replied Big.
"Shit nigga, what he say then?" asked Black.
"He traced Shasta's cell phone to the hotel across the street," replied Big.
"So them hoes been down here balling off my fucking money!" said Black.
"Dat's sho' what it seems like," said Big.
"What room dey staying in?" asked Jason.
"He didn't know, the room isn't registered in either of their names," said Big.
"Well, let's go over there, post up and wait till we see them," said Black.
"Fool, we can't do dat. Be patient. We gone catch dem hoes coming or leaving. We can't get our money if them hoes make a scene, and I damn sho' ain't come all da way to Miami to get banged up. Don't worry, we gone get our fucking money. Promise you dat!" said Jason.
"Now dat we know where they are, we all need to get some rest, we ain't gone be no good if we all tired as hell. That was a long ass drive from Atlanta, plus, dat bitch Shasta real trigger happy and I ain't finna let no bitch catch me slipping 'cause I'm tired," said Jason.
"Man, fuck dat bitch; I'm trigger happy too. Y'all niggas go to sleep, I'm going outside and if I see them I'll ring ya phone," said

Lynise

Black.

Jason and Big go to their room, and Black gets back on the elevator to post up outside. A few hours later, Jason gets a call from a private number. He answers, its Shasta.

"Hello?" asks Jason.

"I got your money and I wanna give it back," said Shasta. When Jason heard it was Shasta's voice on the line he immediately got up out of bed.

"Y'all two bitches got big fucking nuts taking from me," said Jason.

"Listen nigga, I didn't know it was your money, but dat's neither here nor there. I just want you, Big and Black off my fucking back. I'll even give you Kila as interest," said Shasta. At that time Jason was in Big's room with Shasta on speaker phone for him to listen.

"Okay, where are we meeting at? I mean, where are y'all?" asked Jason.

"Nigga, don't play games wit me, I know y'all staying at da Hilton across the street from us," replied Shasta.

"Well, if you know so much, you also know dat we ain't come up here to fucking chat on the damn phone," said Big angrily.

"Imma call you back tomorrow at 6:00 p.m. with an address; till then, enjoy da city," Shasta says and then hangs up and throws the prepaid phone away before Jason or Big could respond.

"Imma murk both of dem bitches real slow, I swear to fucking God, I am!" yells Big angrily.

"Naw, Kila's mine," said Jason. Black walks in the room a few minutes later.

"What's up? Why y'all looking like dat?" asked Black.

"Dat bitch Shasta just called Jason's phone telling him she gone have an address tomorrow fa' us to get our money," said Big.

"But I don't trust dat hoe, we gotta find out where they at before da meeting tomorrow. Aye, Big, call Mr. Iman and see if he can get a location from a blocked number," said Jason.

TWO TIMES BETRAYED

"Aiight," replied Big as he got on the phone and started dialing, he didn't get an answer though.

"It shouldn't be too hard; a hoe is a hoe, no matter what state she in. Hell, we know dem hoes some strippers too, so let's hit every strip club close to they hotel until we find out where they at," said Black.

"Damn it, since they know where we are, we know they won't be stupid enough to come back here," said Jason.

"Y'all niggas gone and suit up, and I'll meet y'all outside," said Black.

It wasn't long before they were all outside, Black had done meet some chic off the strip and she agreed to drive them around and show them the city.

"Aye brah, we down here for business, not pleasure," said Jason.

"Calm down, my nigga; last time I checked, neither one of you know anything 'bout Miami, she just gone show us around and take us to a few spots," said Black.

"What's your name, ma?" asked Big, biting the bottom of his lips, thinking to himself if he was here for pleasure, he wouldn't mind being pleased by her.

"Ella," she replied.

"Aiight, so where to first?" asked Big.

"A friend of mine gotta a lil club up da street from here, y'all will like it," said Ella. Jason studied her and couldn't put a finger on who she reminded him of; with his recent experience with women, he didn't trust them at all. Especially ones he didn't know.

"Then let's go," said Black.

Ella followed behind the men to the car, heading for the passenger side. Jason intervened, giving Ella the keys and telling her to drive; that way it was easier for him to keep an eye on her. Jason wasn't taking any more chances on being tricked by another bitch. Kila had done fucked him up mentally behind her move.

Chapter 19

Shasta and Kila were already outside the club; unbeknownst to Kila, Shasta and Ella had a plan to get rid of Jason, Big, Black, and Kila if everything went accordingly; but like almost all plans, something always goes wrong. Shasta and Kila were supposed to already be inside the club when Ella pulled up with Jason and them. Shasta was gone have Kila in the VIP room waiting for her, and Ella was to make sure that Big and them ended up in the same room. Soon as Shasta saw Jason and them go in, she was to call Nicko and his crew to go in and murk everything. It would've worked out perfectly 'cause Shasta knew that soon as they walked into that VIP room and saw Kila in there, Kila would've, without a second thought, told them that she was there too. As usual, her plan didn't go nowhere near how she wanted it to go. When Ella pulled up with Jason and them, Shasta and Kila were still in line waiting to get inside the club because the new bouncer they had at the door didn't know them, nor did he know Ella when Shasta name dropped her, thinking that would get them in faster. Ella saw them first, she tried to turn around, but Jason spotted Kila second.

"I know damn well dats not dat bitch in line right there!" said Jason. Big and Black look on to see what he's talking about. Jason yells Kila's name and she turns around to face the sound. Ella jumps out the car, leaving her purse and cell phone behind.

"Run, run, run!" yells Ella. Shasta looks up and sees Jason and

Lynise

them running toward them. Ella runs in one direction, Shasta and Kila runs in the other towards the garage were Ella car was parked. It was a distance between the girls and Jason them. Shasta had so many thoughts running through her head, she and Kila were no longer friends, and she wanted desperately for her plan to work so she could get rid of all her problems at one time; but that's not how it ended. Jason and Black got close enough to let shots off. Shasta had the gun that Ella left her before she left. Jason's adrenaline had taken over his rational thinking; he knew he couldn't get money from a dead person, but when he saw Kila, he went into pure rage and didn't even care about the money anymore. He just wanted her dead.

Pop, pop, pop, pop!

Shasta shot back at them.

Pop, pop!

More shots fired, she made it to the garage; however, Kila didn't know one of the rounds caught her in the back. Shasta had made it inside the garage, not noticing she had been hit too; all she felt was a sharp pain in her side. She remembered seeing Nicko and his crew—everything was going so fast. Shasta blacked out, not knowing if she was dead or not. The next morning, Shasta woke up in Mercy General Hospital with a gunshot wound to the abdomen. Just like that, her problems were over; no more Kila, no more Jason and his friends trying to kill her. The police chalked the shootings up to another act of random violence that Miami was known for, and since drugs were found on the victim and in their car, they considered it to be a drug deal gone wrong and did no further investigation. The police didn't even come to the hospital, because Ella had paid the staff off not to report the shooting. Shasta had no emotions behind Kila's death; she accepted the fact that for seven years, she was a friend to Kila; but Kila had never been a friend to her. The doctors wanted her to stay another twenty-four hours for observation before they discharged her. Shasta couldn't wait to get back to Atlanta to see her son. She was ever more ready now to start her life over; as she laid in the hospital bed, she began to day dream of her new beginning. The only obstacle she had left on her list was the upcoming court date for custody she had scheduled with Big Chris. Shasta grabbed the hospital phone to call her aunt. The phone rings. Aunt Nancy's caller ID reads, "Mercy General Hospital" she answers the phone with caution, hoping not to be on the receiving end of bad news.

"Hello?" asks Aunt Nancy.

"Hey auntie," replied Shasta with her voice still hoarse from all the hollering from the previous night.

"Shasta? Is that you?" asked Aunt Nancy.

"Yes, ma'am, it's me. I was just calling to let you know that its all over now and I'll be back in Atlanta tomorrow to get Lil' Chris once I'm discharged from the hospital," replied Shasta.

"Are you okay? Why are you in the hospital? What happened?" asked Aunt Nancy rambling.

"I'm fine, auntie, it's nothing; you don't have to worry about anything. How are you doing though? Have you spoken to my mother?" asks Shasta, hoping that her aunt would just leave it at that because she didn't feel like going over the details of her shooting right now; especially not on the hospital phone.

"I'm okay, just a little bruise that's all; and I spoke with your mother. I didn't tell her anything though, she just wanted to know why you haven't called her; make sure you call her soon. Okay?" said Aunt Nancy.

"I will," said Shasta. Ella walked into the room while she was the phone. She brought flowers and something else wrapped up in a box.

"Oh, yeah auntie, don't tell Lil' Chris I'm coming; I want to surprise him," said Shasta.

"Okay, I won't; take care sweetie, and we will see you soon," said Aunt Nancy. They both hung up. Ella walks toward her to put the flowers on the table and gives her the gift to open. Shasta opens the box to see that it is a brand new cell phone programmed with only five numbers; hers, Nicko's, her mother's, Candace's, and Aunt

Lynise

Nancy's. Shasta just looks at her cousin and smiles. The nurse comes in with another set of flowers from Nicko and places them on the table as well.

"Who died?" joked Shasta.

"Girl, no one who matters; so how you feeling, doll?" asks Ella.

"High," laughs Shasta.

"Nicko and Snoopy are outside in the parking lot, they don't like this hospital shit. You know how men are; but they did tell me to tell you to get well soon and to stay in touch now," said Ella.

"Dat's what's up, girl; I'm ready to get outta here," said Shasta. Ella sits on the bed next to her.

"What a hell of a week; huh?" said Ella.

"Hell, yeah, I could write a book 'bout these last few months of my life," said Shasta.

"So, when do you get outta here?" asked Ella.

"Tomorrow, can you bring my things from the hotel up here? You know what…never mind. I don't want anything, Imma just get to Atlanta, get my son, and start completely over from scratch," Shasta says.

"Starting over is good, you gone stay in Atlanta?" asked Ella.

"Naw, I'm moving for sure. I just don't know where to yet. I was thinking 'bout Virginia or New Jersey. Imma let Lil' Chris pick somewhere. I just hope it's nowhere cold," replied Shasta.

"Well, doll, I dunno when Imma see you again from the looks of it, Miami ain't somewhere you wanna come back to," said Ella.

"Are you kidding? You helped me get my life back lil cuz, and fa' that, I am fa' eva grateful. I will be sure to stay in touch, maybe later when I'm settled, you and Nicko can fly up to see us," said Shasta.

"I would love dat, I love you, and take care of yourself," said Ella.

"I love you too, and you be careful out there," said Shasta.

"You know I will girl," said Ella. She bends down to kiss Shasta on the forehead goodbye, before she leaves, she writes down Mr. Henry's number so he can escort her to the airport once she is discharged. Shasta watches as Ella walks out the room. Ella turns around and waives her cousin bye one last time.

"Till next time, baby cuz," said Shasta quietly to herself. She let the medicine take its course and goes back to sleep 'cause she knows the next time she'd wake up, it would be time to leave Miami.

G STREET CHRONICLES
A LITERARY POWERHOUSE
WWW.GSTREETCHRONICLES.COM

Chapter 20

Shasta's flight landed back in Atlanta round 2:00 p.m., she was standing outside the North terminal waiting on Candace to pick her up. As usual, Candace was late. Shasta pulled out her cell phone Ella had bought her in attempt to call Candace; as she dials, she hears Candace yelling out her name. Shasta lets out a sigh of relief.

"How was your trip, sis?" asked Candace.

"It was fine. More business, than pleasure though," replied Shasta.

"That's cool, at least you gotta chance to get away. I dunno when the last time I been anywhere outside Atlanta," said Candace. Shasta quickly changes the subject in order to avoid getting into a pity party with Candace; she just didn't have the energy for it right now.

"Before we go by Auntie Nancy's, I need you to run me by Amber's house first," said Shasta.

"Okay. Does she still live off 14th Street downtown?" asks Candace.

"Naw, she moved down the street from here, off Riverdale Road," Shasta says.

"I think I know where dats at, just give me directions," said Candace. Shasta nods her head. She sits back in the seat and begins to think of how she was gone get over $300k out of Amber's house.

"Sis? Where I go, I'm on Riverdale," asked Candace.

"Make a right at the Checkers, then make a left on Crystal Lane. Her house is the last one on the right. She gotta broke down green Lexus in her yard." said Shasta.

Lynise

"She stay on the same street Uncle Tommy used to live on; right?" said Candace.

"Yeah, he still live out here on da same street she do," said Shasta.

"Are you gone be here long? 'Cause after I drop you by Auntie Nancy's, I gotta be back to my side of town to get my boys off the after-school bus," said Candace.

"Okay. I just gotta run in here and get something," said Shasta. A few minutes later, they were outside in front of Amber's house, no one was home. Shasta got out the car and walked around to the back of the house. Amber wasn't the brightest chic she knew, so there was a good chance she left something unlock, and she was right. Out of everything she could've left open, it was the side door. Shasta thought to herself, *could this be any easier,* she quickly went inside. Access to the attic was through the hallway; she knew that because her and Uncle Tommy's house were made similar to each other. She grabbed the stool out the living room and reached for the ceiling. A set of stairs came down, Shasta climbed them and began searching for her money. She used the light from her phone to guide her as she poked holes in every wall up there, when she got to the last one on the side of the window, she saw a black trash bag fall on the floor. She stuck her hand through the wall to feel the contents of bag; when she felt that it was her money, she vandalized the rest of the wall to get it out.

"How in the hell did that bitch get this bag back here in the first place?" asked Shasta…talking to herself. She didn't notice the vent above her head where Kila had dropped the money down. Shasta got the trash bag out the wall and quickly made her way back to Candace's car.

"Pop your trunk," said Shasta. Shasta threw the trash bag inside the trunk.

"You straight, sis?" asks Candace.

"Yeah, I'm good," answers Shasta as she gets back in the car.

"How's your stomach?" asked Candace. Shasta looked at her with a confused face.

TWO TIMES BETRAYED

"Who told you, how you know I got shot?" asked Shasta hoping her mother didn't know considering how Candace runs her mouth.

"That doesn't matter, sis. Look, I know lately me and you haven't been seeing eye to eye, but your still my sister. You're the only sister I got, and it would kill me if anything happen to you. I love you," said Candace.

Shasta stared at her sister as she spoke, it's been a while since she heard her be serious about anything.

"I love you too, baby girl. I'm fine though, just a lil pain every now and then. It ain't nothing oxycodone can't cure," jokes Shasta.

"I bet Lil' Chris is gone be so happy to see you," said Candace.

"I know. I can't wait to see him either, it's been over a month since I last saw him, and he don't even know I'm back yet. I told Auntie Nancy not to tell 'em, I wanna surprise him," said Shasta. Candace takes her hand and lovingly rubs it across her sister's face.

"Are you done with that life now?" asked Candace.

"I sure am, sis. No more clubs, no more long nights and finally, no more Kila," said Shasta, sighing with relief.

"So, what you gone do now that your back in Atlanta?" asked Candace.

"Well. sis, dats hard to say since I don't plan on being in Atlanta too much longer either," said Shasta.

"Auntie Nancy mentioned that. Do you know where you wanna go as of now?" asked Candace.

"Not yet, Imma let Lil' Chris pick somewhere for us. Auntie Nancy bought him a map for me, so I'll know as soon as I get there," said Shasta. Soon they were pulling up in front of Aunt Nancy's house.

"Tell Aunt Nancy I can't come in, 'cause I'm in a rush, but Imma see her Sunday for church," said Candace. Shasta gets out the car, grabs her bag out of the trunk and walks over to the driver's side of the car. She reaches in the bag and takes out a band of money.

"Huh, sis, this should help you out a little with da new baby," said Shasta. Candace looks at all the money.

Lynise

"Oh, my gosh, sis; how much is this?" asked Candace.

"I'm not sure, maybe a lil over ten thousand," replied Shasta. Candace gets out the car and gives her sister a big hug.

"Thank you, thank you so much. You just don't know how bad I really needed this. I wanted to ask for your help, I just didn't know how. Thank you, Shasta," said Candace as her eyes began to water with tears.

"Just promise me you won't let your boyfriend spend it for you," said Shasta.

"You don't have to worry about him anymore, I put 'em out around the same time you left. Trust me when I say I'm done with him and everyone else who don't mean me or mines any good," said Candace as she got back in the car. They said their goodbyes once more and Shasta looks on as she watches her baby sister pull out the driveway.

"See you later, sis." said Shasta to herself, for she knows it would be a minute before she saw her sister again.

Chapter 21

Shasta sat on the front porch a few minutes before she rang the door bell, as she sat on the steps, her mind took her back to the first time she met Kila. Shasta was eighteen and had been away from home for almost a year, and Kila was seventeen and going from house to house using fake IDs to dance at Loop's and other strip clubs throughout the city. In the beginning it was like they were all each other had; their families didn't understand them, or what they were trying to accomplish. Both of them wanted a better life, both of them wanted to get out of the hood, and for the sacrifice of many nights they did. As the years went on, they became different people with different views on life. Shasta was thankful that, that chapter in her life was finally over; as she stood up to ring the doorbell she felt her phone vibrating. It was her mother, she knew Ella had done called her to let know she had made it back; hell, Ella probably had already called everyone, she laughed to herself. Even though Shasta wasn't ready to talk to her mother yet, she answered her phone anyway.

"Hey, mommy," said Shasta.

"Hey, stranger," said her mother.

"I've been meaning to call you, sweetie; anyway how are you?" asked Shasta.

"I'm fine. I should be asking you that though," said her mother.

"I'm better now," said Shasta, hoping that Candace or Ella hadn't

Lynise

told her mother that she had been shot. She absolutely didn't feel like discussing that right now. There was a brief silence before her mother spoke again.

"I- I need to tell you something, sweetie," said her mother. Shasta could hear the cracks in her mother's voice as she spoke; she sounded the same way she did when she gave her the news of her grandmother passing.

"What's wrong?" asked Shasta nervously.

"You remember a couple months ago you called to tell me dat Lil' Chris' daddy was taking you to court?" asked her mother.

"Yes, ma'am. Why?" asked Shasta.

"Well, I sent my problem solver out to his house to see if he could get 'em to change his mind or at least come to a better understanding about things, ya know," said her mother.

"Uh, huh, so what happened?" asked Shasta.

"Well, um, when he went got there, they had his house blocked off with yellow tape. They say it was a home invasion; his wife found him dead with a bullet to the back of his head," said her mother.

"Oh, shit, fa' real ma? Do they know who did it?" asked Shasta.

"Naw, they didn't say. It was on the news and everything," said her mother. Shasta knew who was responsible for Big Chris's death, they were all dead too. Shasta's relationship with Big Chris was bitter, and she had no love for him. He had mistreated her so much during the time they were together and it had only gotten worse once they'd split; so when her mother told her the news, she wasn't sad. Her heart was heavy because she didn't know how she was going to tell her son; Lil' Chris adored his father. For that reason alone, her eyes began to water.

"Shasta? Will you be okay?" asked her mother.

"Yes ma'am, Imma be fine, just trying to figure out how Imma tell Lil' Chris he will never see his father again. Ma, he's only four years old. I don't wanna do that to him," said Shasta as tears rolled down her face.

TWO TIMES BETRAYED

"Baby, my advice to you, give it couple days and let everything process. You get your son, move and get settled into your new place, new state or whatever you plan to do now that your back. Then once your settled, you sit Lil' Chris down and tell him about his father. There was nothing you could've done to prevent this, home invasions are happening often these days," said her mother. Shasta wiped her face and pulled herself together, she didn't want to go around her son looking stressed out or sad.

"Umph. Okay, I will, once we're settled. I'm at Aunt Nancy's house now. Imma come by and see you before we leave. I gotta surprise for you too, but Imma leave it with Auntie Nancy for her to give you when she see you in church Sunday," said Shasta.

"Shasta, everything gone be okay. You're a strong women and you've come a long way. I'm very proud of you, there's no looking back now, sweetie. I love you, baby girl and Imma talk to you later."

"I love you too, bye bye." said Shasta and she hung up. Shasta rang the door bell.

"Who is it?" said Auntie Nancy as she peeped through the window.

"It's me, Auntie," said Shasta. Aunt Nancy opened the door, a huge smile embraced her face once she saw Shasta.

"Praise God. Hey, sweetheart! When did you get back? How did you get here? Me and George would've picked you up from the airport,." said Aunt Nancy as she hugged Shasta.

"Oh, it's okay Auntie. Candace picked me up; she told me to tell y'all hey. She was in a rush to pick her boys up on time," said Shasta.

"Where are your bags? Come in, come in, Christopher will be so happy to see you. He's in the family room with Uncle George. I was just making lunch. Are you hungry?" asked Aunt Nancy still rambling in excitement to see her.

"Naw, I'm fine. I'm not really that hungry, I had a snack on the plane. Imma take Lil' Chris out to eat or something now that I'm back," said Shasta. The bruise on Auntie Nancy's face had seemed to heal fine, it was hardly noticeable with makeup on. Shasta followed

Lynise

Aunt Nancy to the kitchen.

"Christopher!" hollered Aunt Nancy. "Guess who's here!"

Christopher came running into the kitchen, he sees his mother and jumps into her arms. Shasta tries hard to hold back tears, but she can't. This time they were tears of joy.

"Hi, baby." said Shasta.

"Hey, mommy!" said Lil' Chris in happiness to see his mother.

"I missed you so, so…so much!" said Shasta as she kisses her son repeatedly on the forehead. She puts him down to look at him; this was the longest she'd ever been away from him. Her stomach was hurting a little, but she didn't care. All she cared about was seeing the smile on Lil' Chris's face.

"Look at you, big man, you've grown so much. I'm not gone be able to pick you up soon, son," said Shasta jokingly.

"Auntie Nan been making me eat spinach. Mommy, I hate eating spinach! When we move, don't buy dat," said Lil' Chris. Shasta and Aunt Nancy just looked at him and laugh. Uncle George enters the kitchen to greet Shasta. He sits at the table to observe the bond between Christopher and his mother.

"Guess what, mommy?" asked Lil' Chris.

"What baby?" replied Shasta.

"Auntie Nan bought me a map!" said Lil' Chris in excitement.

"Oh, she did. Well, did you pick a new state for us to move to?" asked Shasta.

"I sure did. We moving to Kon-kit-at-kit," said Lil' Chris. They all laughed at the mispronunciation of the state Connecticut.

"Where?" smiled Shasta.

"He means, Connecticut," said Uncle George smiling.

"What's so special about Connecticut?" asked Shasta.

"I dunno, I just like the name," replied Lil' Chris. Laughter filled the kitchen.

"Then Connecticut it is baby!" said Shasta. She watched as her son spun around on the kitchen floor in excitement.

TWO TIMES BETRAYED

"Auntie Nancy, I need one more favor from you," said Shasta.

"Sure. What is it, dear?" asked Aunt Nancy. She reached in the trash bag and pulled out four bands of money totaling over $40k.

"Can you split this between you and my mother?" asked Shasta.

Auntie Nancy and Uncle George looked at all the money she placed on the counter.

"Baby, you don't have to do this, you're my first niece. You're like a daughter to me, payment isn't necessary," said Aunt Nancy. Uncle George cleared his throat in disagreement still staring at all the money. He walks over, closer to Shasta.

"Hush, Nancy, she knows she ain't have to do this, but since she did, ain't nothing wrong with putting it to good use. Shasta, sweetheart, Imma make sure Gloria get her cut. Hell, your uncle need him a new set of golf clubs," said Uncle George. Shasta laughs at her uncle 'cause she would've been on the same shit when it came to that money.

"Aiight, baby boy, go get your things. We have so much to do before we leave," said Shasta. Uncle George grabs the money off the table and leaves to go help Lil' Chris pack. Aunt Nancy and Shasta watches as they leave the kitchen.

"Do you mind dropping us off at the house, I'm really not up for small talk right now if we catch a cab," said Shasta.

"Of course I will sweetie," replied Aunt Nancy.

"Thank you." said Shasta.

"My pleasure," said Aunt Nancy. She reaches in the drawer and pulls out a manila business card. Aunt Nancy hands it to Shasta. The card reads, Eveyln Moore Realties.

"When Lil' Chris told me he wanted to move to Connecticut, I gave Evelyn a call and she helped me find a cute starter apartment for you. It's a month-to-month lease agreement. I paid your rent up for three months to give you enough time to find you and Lil' Chris a house," said Aunt Nancy. Shasta looks at her auntie in amazement; no one had ever done anything close to something like this for her before.

Lynise

"As soon as you get up there and get settled, give her a call and the two of you can go from there," says Aunt Nancy. Shasta walks over to her aunt and gives her a long hug.

"What would I do without you, Auntie?" asked Shasta as she still hugs her aunt.

"I dunno, my sweet. Let's hope we don't have to find out anytime soon," said Aunt Nancy. Uncle George and Lil' Chris reappear back in the kitchen with his things.

"Are you ready lil man?" asked Shasta.

"Yes sir ree!" said Lil' Chris in excitement.

Uncle George walks them outside, he hugs Shasta and Lil' Chris goodbye. They get in the car and drive off.

They arrived at Shasta's apartment a half hour later due to the excessive traffic.

"So, when are you leaving?" asked Aunt Nancy.

"In a few days. I need to go home and pack and call movers for my furniture. Then Imma go see my mother before we leave too," said Shasta.

"Mommy. Can I bring some toys with us on da airplane?" asked Lil' Chris

"Sure honey, but not too many, okay," replied Shasta.

"Well, I guess this is it Auntie, on to a new beginning. I have so much to do. I will call you once we get to Kon-kit-at-kit," said Shasta, imitating Lil' Chris.

Aunt Nancy hugged her once more before she got out the car.

"I love you and thank you for everything. I really mean it." said Shasta.

"Oh…I love you too." said Aunt Nancy.

"I love you too, Aunt Nan!" said Lil' Chris.

"Right back at cha," said Aunt Nancy as she turned around to hive five Lil' Chris. Shasta and her son get out the car and waive Aunt Nancy goodbye.

Shasta grabs Lil' Chris with one hand, and the trash bag full of money in the other and walks towards the elevators. She sees a note on the wall that reads: *On behalf of Atlantic Station Management and our wonderful tenants. We would like to thank the Atlanta Police Department for their success in apprehending the criminal who was responsible for many stalkings and several rape attempts in this community and neighboring ones. Job well done! Below was a picture of the culprit and his truck.*

The description was of a white, older looking male in his late thirties, early forties, and a black, SUV with tinted windows. Shasta studies the picture and lets out a sigh of relief, because she knew that the person apprehended by the police was the same man following her.

"Are you ready to start our new life, son?" asked Shasta.

"Yes, ma'am! I can't wait!" replied Lil' Chris.

"So am I," said Shasta. She hugs her son and gets on the elevators.

G STREET CHRONICLES
A LITERARY POWERHOUSE
WWW.GSTREETCHRONICLES.COM

PART TWO

"GREED WAS JUST THE BEGINNING, NOW ITS REVENGE"

G STREET CHRONICLES
A LITERARY POWERHOUSE
WWW.GSTREETCHRONICLES.COM

Introduction

None needed. Just read, enjoy and by all means try to keep up. For, some situations in life will throw yo' ass in the blender every time.

"What goes up, will come down, and some people it's best to stay the fuck from around."

-Shasta

G STREET CHRONICLES
A LITERARY POWERHOUSE
WWW.GSTREETCHRONICLES.COM

Chapter 1

Two Years After Kila

If I could go back in time, I probably wouldn't change a thing. My experience in life is what made me who I am today. Although, it's been a long, hectic road, I'm exactly where I want to be in life.

Those were the thoughts Shasta constantly self-assured herself of on a daily basis since her relocation from Atlanta to Connecticut. Even through success, she always found herself thinking about the past events of her life. How if she would have just told Kila "No" that night, maybe her best friend of ten years would've never betrayed her and would be six feet on top of ground instead of below it. Maybe her son's father would still be alive. Maybe she wouldn't have left the only home she ever knew. Who knows?

Time doesn't heal a damn thing; it just makes you grow more numb and guarded. At this point in Shasta's life, she most definitely wasn't open to trusting anyone.

Interrupted in deep thought, Shasta was startled by the ring of her cell phone. She walked over to the counter only to see it was her sister, Candace, calling.

"Hello?" said Shasta.

"Hey, sis? I ain't think you would be up this early," said Candace.

"Yeah, girl, I'm up. Lil' Chris had a sleep over last night, so you know they had my ass up bright an early," laughed Shasta.

Lynise

"Dats kids for ya."

"What's up with ya though? I was just sitting here thinking 'bout you. Ain't nobody heard from you in a minute now. We miss you down here," Candace said.

"I miss y'all too."

"I just been busy as fuck."

"I can't believe it's been two years since I left Atlanta," Shasta replied.

"I know right, time done went by so fast."

"When you coming back down to visit? I wanna see my nephew, and you know Mama and Auntie Nancy wanna see y'all too."

" Done got up there and now you act like you don't know no damn body," Candace rambles on as she always did.

"Shit girl, I dunno yet."

"I'm just now getting settled. Lil' Chris just now getting situated. He finally stopped asking to see his daddy. My club is taking off, I promise to come visit soon, love."

"Speaking of Lil' Chris. How is my nephew liking the change of scenery?"

"Girl, he's adapting well, he getting big as fuck."

" Can you believe my baby about to be six years old?"

"Hell, girl, I'm still in awe that yo' ass even got a baby. I had three babies before Lil' Chris was even four," Laughed Candace.

"Whatever."

" I wasn't in no rush." Laughed Shasta, walking to the back porch to check on Lil' Chris and his company, the neighbor's kids Ryan and his younger brother Zack.

"Miracle!" Hollering with the phone still to her mouth.

"Bring me Mya's bottle," yelled Candace to her oldest daughter.

Shasta had to pull the phone away from her ear as she thought to herself, *my sister is ghetto as hell.*

"How old is Miracle now, Candi?"

"Her grown ass will be fourteen in May."

TWO TIMES BETRAYED

"Damn, she getting up there. She will be eighteen before you know it."

"If she lives to see her 18th birthday. Imma fuck around and stomp her smart mouthed ass da fuck out."

"Bitch, you were grown as fuck too, hell you saying?" responded Shasta.

"And you know her grown ass fucking too," Candace said, trying to jump subject.

"I got off work early one day last month and she had some lil nigga in my got damn bed! Outta all the places, this bitch gettin' bent over in my damn room. Girl, I tried to throw dat freaky heffa out da damn window. If it wasn't fo Ms. Laura, I'd probably be in damn jail right now," Shasta could hear the change in her sister's tone of voice as if that shit just happened yesterday.

"Shit. She ain't no different from how your ass used to be from when we was coming up. I remember Mama used to be two steps away from going to jail too," laughed Shasta.

"Shitting' me. I was the good child."

"No hell yo' ass wasn't. Mama did always say that what we did when we was young would come back on us ten times over through our kids."

"Well, boo. You fucked. You for sure gone have your hands full with Lil' Chris then. We all know you were the furthest from being a saint."

"Whatever!"

"Whatever, my ass." Candace laughed again.

"Anyway love, as much as I would love to stay on the phone with yo' ass and chat, I gotta get myself together and get ready for today."

"What's on da agenda? Knowing you…you always got something going on." "Same ol'. Gotta take my ass to da grocery store before Lil' Chris and his friends eat me out of house and home. I got to interview three more dancers to replace the three I had to fire last week for dat messy shit. Clearly, after all I done been through with bitches, I ain't

Lynise

with da sneaky shit no mo'."

"Damn, Ms. Thing, yo' club doing numbers like dat? Send me a check, I could always use some extra cash love," laughed Candace.

Shasta completely ignored Candace last statement. Her lil sister always wanted or needed something. It wasn't like she ain't send money down there every month for her, her Mama and especially Auntie Nancy.

"Of course, doll. This me who you talking to. Imma have to fuck around and buy the empty space next door to just make room for da muthafuckas who be complaining 'bout never getting in cause the lines be round da corner."

"Shit, if they ass became members like da rest, they wouldn't have that problem. I gotta 'em though. Anyway that's another conversation."

"Well, you will figure out something, honey, you always do."

"I know something will give."

"Well, sis, Imma let you gone and get your day started. I know you hear these bad ass kids in da background turning up. Imma call you lata tonight or tomorrow."

"Aiight, baby girl. I love you. Talk to you lata."

"Love you tooooooo!"

They both hung the phone.

Once again, Shasta caught herself reflecting 'bout the years before. How shit can really go sour fast as fuck and how your so-called friends could be the very ones having your family going to your funeral if you let 'em catch you slipping. Shasta quickly shook off the fucked up memories and got back to focusing on the now. Still feeling slick drained from last night, Shasta headed to the kitchen to make her some coffee laced with five-hour energy. Looking at all the dishes in the sink she attempted to load the dishwasher, then changed her mind.

"Ahhh! I need a fucking maid. I'm way too busy for this shit," yelled Shasta, talking to her kitchen like it would respond.

TWO TIMES BETRAYED

Ranting and raving Shasta felt like if she wasn't working, she was cleaning up after Lil' Chris. So that meant she was always working.

Even though Shasta loved her huge new house, at the same time it was just too big for her to maintain on regular basis by herself. She lived in and rather upscale neighborhood—gated community of course. She had a 5,000 square foot, Georgian-style home with five bedrooms and 4.5 bathrooms. It was built with a finished basement, equipped with a gym and full-size bar. It had original custom moldings and fixtures and a formal living room with cathedral ceilings. Her kitchen was state of the art. Customly designed by Aderi', with burnt cherry wood cabinets and beautiful American-made granite counter tops, her house also sat on a nice piece of land, large enough for the custom-made playground she had built for Lil' Chris in the backyard. The pool she also had built in the shape of a money bag, she kept empty and covered up until Lil' Chris was ready to learn how to swim. It was just gorgeous. Especially compared to the small place she had when she first moved to Connecticut. Money sure enough was good up north and her club was becoming more and more successful every night.

Shasta grabs her cell phone, this time to call Ryan and Zack's momma, Ariel. The phone rings and the voicemail comes on.

"Hey. You've reached Ariel, leave a message at the beep."

Shasta left a message.

"Hey, girl, this Shasta. Can I please borrow Ms. Lucy? Call me back when you get this. Bye."

Ariel and Shasta were around the same age. Ariel got her check like most single women had in their neighborhood. Through either divorce or inheritance; Ariel's situation was divorce. She decided to surprise her husband at work one day and caught him fucking a temp in his office. *We all know the rest.* To make a long story short, that muthafucka gone be cutting da check for a while, and then some.

So far, Shasta and Ariel were cool. Shasta loved Ariel's Texan accent. She was the first white girl she really ever kicked it with outside the club. Ariel also kept an eye on Lil' Chris for her when she was at her club most nights.

Shasta was really hands on when it came to her club, "Luxury" one of Connecticut's hottest gentlemen's clubs. She doubled checked everything all the time, especially when it came to her money. Shit, she had been there, done that. Wasn't in the game for loses this go round. Business was good.

Shasta's phone rings. It's Ariel returning her call.

"Hello."

"Well, hello darling," Ariel said in the Texan accent Shasta loved.

"I was calling to see if I could borrow Ms. Lucy again. My house is a fucking mess."

"You sure may. I don't know why you just don't call that service I gave you months back."

"I been meaning too, doll."

"Uh, huh."

"What them boys of mine been up to? I sho' hope they ain't been giving you a hard time."

"Naw, girl they fine. Those boys of yours are so adorable. They all in the backyard playing and throwing shit last time I looked in on 'em," Shasta laughed.

"Well, that's sho' is good to hear."

"Do you gotta work tonight?" asked Ariel.

"And you know it. All work and no play."

"Tell me about it. Well, Imma send Ms. Lucy right on over. Leave your key for her to lock up when she done. Lil' Chris can spend the night over here with the boys."

" Okay, cool. Thanks."

"Soon as I get some free time, Imma have to take you some where real nice. You have been such a good friend to me since I been here and I really appreciate it."

"Now don't go getting all mushy on me, plus, as far as I know it, darling, I'm your only friend," joked Ariel.

TWO TIMES BETRAYED

"Ha, ha. I guess you are."

"I would love to continue this conversation, love, but I gotta run doll."

"Pierre is at my door and you know I refuse to miss my hour yoga session with that fine drink of water."

"Smooches." Ariel said.

"Right back at ya," Shasta aid as she hung the phone.

G STREET CHRONICLES
A LITERARY POWERHOUSE
WWW.GSTREETCHRONICLES.COM

CHAPTER 2

Club Luxury

Shasta pulled up in front of her club listening to none other than her daily favorite Young Jeezy. His new joint R.I.P featuring 2 Chainz was the shit. She played that song so much you would've thought she wrote and produced it. This was her daily routine, Monday through Saturday and Sunday's were designated for Lil' Chris. Shasta sat inside her car and rolled up the last little bit of Loud she had stuffed inside of her glove compartment. Happy hour was about to jump off inside the club. Her bouncer/security was there standing at the entrance watching her, waiting for her to get out of the car. She took a few more pulls off her blunt, and then got out to greet Stacey.

"Imma have to give Stacey a lil more responsibility," she said out loud to herself as she walked toward her club—music blasting so loud you could hear it in the parking lot.

"What's up, Ms. Shasta. How it's treating you so far this afternoon?" asked Nick, her bouncer guarding the entrance of Luxury as if his life depended on it.

Nick was a huge ass nigga, originally from South Carolina. He stood every bit of six feet and a solid 300 pounds—black as hell. Well-known in da club world for putting niggas on they back; so of course, no one fucked with him, or fucked up around him for that matter.

Lynise

"Hey Nick. It's cooling. How you?"

"Good, good."

"Dats good to hear, I know you got it together out here." Shasta proceeded inside her club.

Luxury was an upscale gentlemen's club. Very, very nice, it had ten stages and six bars. Ten Fun Rooms equipped with shower swings and wall mirrors. Bose amplified surround sound throughout the building. Fish tanks in each of the walls. It put you in the mind of da Flame down south, just way bigger. It was beautiful. A man's paradise and the clientele was anyone from doctors to big-time dope boys.

It was *members only*, which fell into two categories: Gold & VIP. The Gold members paid a $300 membership fee monthly, while the VIP's paid $500 with three months paid up front from the both of them. Shasta thought it was best to run her club like this, because it kept out a lot of broke ass niggas and bitches from just walking in. Buying one drink, thinking they finna stare at free pussy all night. Shasta had it sat up to where you were guaranteed to spend money and the girls were guaranteed to make it. She charged her new dancers a house rent of $150 till they got they feet wet, and the vets $200 a night. On any night, she had about thirty to forty dancers in the club. Shasta also did the interviewing herself; unlike most, she had to make sure her clients were getting top notch quality and variety. If you worked for Shasta, you made money; if you didn't, something was wrong with you and you weren't working for her much longer.

The waitresses made their money off memberships if clients chose to sit in their designated area. The bartenders made stupid money because Shasta gave free memberships to Steelwood Brewer & Exchange CEO and Exec's. One of the East Coast biggest liquor and wine distributors, so of course, no cocktail was over $10. Even the bouncer's were jugging, they charged $300 at da door to let niggas get in if they wasn't a member. Shasta knew. She ain't trip, she figured if they would spend $300 just to get in per night, they will keep spending, 'cause her girls weren't no low-budget, cheap ass

TWO TIMES BETRAYED

dancers. What choice did they have?

Everyone who loved pussy, loved Shasta's club. It had so many perks. The memberships came with what Shasta loved to call "The Fun Room" which gave each Gold member one hour twice a month with any girl of their choice. VIP's got the same thing only they were able to indulge four times a month with two girls. Anything goes, and they must be XTRA generous, plus, Shasta got to charge $5 a minute 'cause she knew what went on in the fun rooms. Long as the girls were willing…and 98% of them were…no questions were asked.

"Don't you just loooove happy hour?"

Shasta turned around to see who it was talking to her. It was a newbie named Maui, an Asian American girl she had just hired last week. Maui was a little bitty thing standing about 5'6' and that was with heels on. She had jet black hair down to her ass; slim, petite figure, proudly exposing a new pair of recently bought 36C's her last sponsor bought her. She wore red contacts that gave her that gothic poison look. It was hot, and for her to barely been at Luxury a week she was already bringing in $2,000 a night before house rent. Once she established and solid consistent request list she would be considered a vet. The way it looked, she would be getting promoted real soon.

"Baby doll, I love just about anything that makes me money."

Maui followed Shasta to the elevators to her upstairs office overlooking the club.

"Me too," Maui said, still following Shasta to her office which was also guarded at all times too.

"Good afternoon, Ma'am," said Security.

"Hello," replied Shasta to her security whose name was Big Mo, ex-military who also stood in stature the same as Nick only difference is he had 45 caliber tucked away in the back of his shirt. Shasta tapped her card and entered her office with Maui still following close behind her. Shasta didn't have a problem with Maui clinging to her the way she did. She remembered being eighteen and carefree once upon a time. Shasta thought it was cute.

Lynise

"So, is Future still performing tonight?" asked Maui.

"Of course, he is." Shasta took a seat at her desk going over last night numbers, making sure everything added up.

"I can't wait to meet him. I just love, love his music!" Maui said excitedly looking down at the rest of the club through Shasta's two-way mirror on the floor.

"Yeah, he's real cool. You will like him, he's been here a few times," Shasta was still focused at her laptop.

"Do me a favor and go get me a drink please. Have Melody to make it for me."

"Okay. What do want to drink?" asked Maui, just as bubbly as hell.

"Um...I dunno. Surprise me." Shasta still did not look up to take her eyes off the last of the bank statements.

"K."

Maui disappeared downstairs and went straight to the bar. No stops in between.

"I see you still following Ms. Shasta around," said Carmen sarcastically.

"Jealous, it seems," replies Maui.

"Psst...Not at all, that's what puppies do. They follow their owners, wagging their tails in high hopes of a treat."

"FUCK YOU!" Maui said as she flicked her middle finger at Carmen, leaving her end of the bar headed over to Melody's side.

From the expression on Maui's face, Melody knew Carmen was fucking with her again.

"Don't pay her no mind, girl; Carmen acts like that with all the newbies."

"Shit please, I ain't studying her, honey!"

"Anyway Ms. Shasta would like for you to make her a drink."

"She say what she want?"

"She told me to tell you to surprise her," Maui Giggled.

"Aiight, aiight. Melody's Special coming up."

TWO TIMES BETRAYED

"Um, okay. I hope she likes it. Mata fact make me one first just to test it out for her."

"Ha, ha cute. I make this for her all the time. Maui just say you wanna taste it," smiled Melody as she poured her a sample in a shot glass.

"It's good."

"I know."

Melody gave Maui, Shasta's drink along with one for herself. Maui left Melody a $10 tip then headed back to elevators. She felt the strange feeling someone was watching so she turned around. Indeed it was Carmen staring so hard she could've burned a hole straight through her outfit. Clearly ignoring the nigga in front of her waiting to be served. Funny. Maui blew her a kiss and got on the elevator, before the doors closed Carmen returned the gesture Maui gave earlier an shot her bird with both hands. Maui laughed. Melody walked over to Carmen's end with her hands on her hips.

"Tell me why you always fucking with that damn girl. She ain't even been here a full week yet. What she do to you that damn fast?" Melody asks.

Carmen looked at Melody like she was asking her to pay her damn rent or something.

"Cause I just damn don't. What the fuck. I ain't gotta like everybody yo' ass do."

"Yo' crazy ass don't like no damn body."

"Naw, I just don't like her ass."

"And why not?"

"What does it matter to you? Take yo' ass back to yo end of the bar—friend police."

"You need help." Melody stated.

"And you need to keep yo' ass over there on your end cuz you can get it to."

"Whatever," Melody replied as she walked off.

Shasta sat watching Maui walk back towards her office through

Lynise

her security monitor. She buzzed her in before she got the chance to knock on the door.

"Here you go," said Maui, handing Shasta her drink then bowing after, going back to her Japanese culture.

"What creation in a glass she made for me this time?" Shasta asked before she took a sip.

"Melody's Special," Maui replied with a big smile on her face. "It tastes good too," Maui said, taking her drink to da head.

"Good choice. It's one of my favorite drinks."

"What exactly is a "Melody Special" anyway?"

"It's um, Tequila, Rose', pineapple juice and Rose's limeade over fine crushed ice."

"Well, I like it. She should put this goodness in a bottle." Maui plopping down on Shasta's dark green cashmere couch imported straight from Italy as a gift from the Mayor.

"What's going with you and Carmen? Shasta asked.

Maui looked at Shasta with the how da fuck you know that face. Shasta simply pointed to the camera's rewinding back to the shooting of the birds between them.

"Don't lie," Shasta said firmly.

"Ms. Shasta I really don't know. I ain't never done nothing to her."

"Um, okay."

Shasta's intercom buzzed and from the look on Maui's face she was glad it did. It was Stacey.

"What's up?"

"Some chick outside is really stressing to Nick 'bout she got an interview with you today. You ain't tell me 'bout no interview. What happen with the other two girls you supposed to be interviewing? Are they still coming?"

"Slow down girl, damn. Tell him to have Carmen escort her up. And for the other 300 hundred questions you just asked me in two seconds. Nothing, I rescheduled them. I decided to let you interview them. It's about time I gave you some more responsibility, don't you think?"

"That's what I been trying to tell you for the longest."

A few minutes later, Valerie was walking into the club. She looked around so fascinated, the average eye would think this was the first strip club she had ever been in. Little did they know she wasn't in there two minutes and had already counted fourteen cameras including the eight that were outside covering the parking lot.

Stacey introduced herself and then walked Valerie over to the bar to be escorted to Shasta's office by Carmen.

"Shasta's said bring her upstairs." Stacey said to Carmen.

"Okay."

Stacey walked off in direction to the locker rooms. Even though Stacey had done her share of shaking it around bucked-naked, she was still sexy as fuck; retired or not. *Hot Stacey* is what the members called her. She stood 5'7"; a redbone with short cut sandy brown hair. Thick with it. Old school, open-face golds on her bottom grill. Rocking a big ass tattoo of a cherry dripping down the center of her back headed straight to the crack of her ass. She was in charge of the day-to-day settings of the club when Shasta was away. If you needed to see Shasta, nine times outta ten, you went through her first.

Shasta saw Carmen and Valerie getting on to the elevator. Big Mo was holding the door open for them as they got off. The ladies walk in, Shasta greets them. Carmen attempts to leave.

"Carmen, you stay as well."

Looking confused on why Shasta wants her to stay, Carmen has no choice but to sit next to Maui on the couch. Shasta turns her attention to Valerie and extends her hand.

"I'm Shasta Davis," she introduces herself.

"Valerie Alexis Carter."

"Well, turn around and let me see if you look anything like the pictures on your profile," Shasta said.

Valerie did as told.

"Nice so far, now undress."

Lynise

Valerie nervously started taking off her clothes piece by piece. She turned around again at Shasta's request so she could view the back end of her beauty. This chick was fine as fuck, golden caramel complexion, hazel contact free eyes, Nicki Minaj ass with small perky B-Cup titties. To top it off she had tattoo of an African black panther crawling up her leg from her calf in direction to her pussy.

"My members will love you."

"You can start tonight if you want," Shasta impressed excitement about how much money this new addition to team could bring her.

"That's it?" asked Valerie with a look of confusion and being caught off guard because she didn't expect to be hired on the spot.

"Yep that's it. Any questions?"

"Um, no."

"Okay good. Big Mo gone take you back down stairs and hand you over to Stacey. She's the club manager, any questions or concerns you can go to her. She'll fill you in on the do's and don'ts and also your nightly obligation. It was very nice to meet you. I'm sure you will do fine."

Valerie put back on her clothes and went to meet Big Mo at the door.

"One more thing, file this paperwork out and be sure to give it to Stacey before you get on the floor."

"Welcome to Luxury. I'm confident you'll love it here just as well as everyone else does."

"Thank you Ms. Davis."

"Call me Ms. Shasta, and you're welcome. Now get out there and make us some money love."

"Imma come down a lil lata to check on you before I leave, but I know your be in good hands with Stacey."

"Okay," Valerie replied, leaving out of Shasta's office.

"Now for you two, I don't know what the beef is and I really don't care." Shasta directed her comments toward Carmen and Maui who were still sitting on her couch. Carmen attempted to interrupt.

TWO TIMES BETRAYED

"Carmen don't interrupt me. I'm not through speaking yet."

Shasta downed the rest of her Melody's Special.

"As I was saying. I don't know what the fuck up with y'all two, but I do know I don't need that bullshit here in my club. Carmen you been here the longest, so you of all know how this shit go first hand. Whatever it is, y'all either fix it or stay da fuck away from each other. If it's that serious you are both free to sign up for fight night next weekend. Am I clear?"

"As water, Ms. Shasta," said Carmen.

Maui just sat there and nodded innocently.

"Okay then, we done. Now both of y'all go get back to da money. We got a lot of horny, thirsty, members down there," laughed Shasta.

They both got up and started to leave her office.

"Carmen, you go first. I'd hate to fire one of my best bartenders and my money-making newbie for fighting in the elevator," Shasta said in a more serious tone this time.

"Sure," Carmen replied . You could see the steam coming off her body.

A few seconds later, Carmen was back at the bar. Shasta could tell she was forcing a smile, but she ain't give a fuck as long as her customers were taking care of. She knew she would get over it, especially when she got back into her "I'm gone get my paper zone" which happened sooner than later.

Still standing there, watching Carmen through the monitors do her thing at the bar. Maui felt it was her time to exit Shasta's office as well.

"And for you? You cool, you may even have a future here but all that could quickly change if you can't co-exist with the other girls."

"Confusion don't make nobody no money."

"I understand Ms. Shasta."

"Aiight now baby girl, don't eva let no bullshit get in the way of your check. Speaking of check, Stacey texted me and said you got your first "Fun Room" request in twenty minutes. It's a VIP member, so you make sure you treat him nice."

Lynise

"Okay. I'll make sure he's taken care of." Maui attempted to leave again.

"One more thing before you go, bring me up another Melody's Special…two."

"Aiight."

Shasta sat back in her chair and watched Maui as she left her office. Moments later Maui returned with Shasta's drinks.

"Thanks, doll."

"My pleasure."

"Now go get that money!" stated Shasta in a more relaxed mode after taking a few sips of her cocktail.

"Yes, ma'am!" Maui saluted Shasta as if she was in the military.

They both burst out into laughs.

"Girl, get yo' ass outa here," Shasta said still laughing.

Once again, Maui was gone. Shasta watched her via her security monitors she paid so close attention to and from the looks of it, Shasta's pep talk about bullshit and paper had her skipping to the dressing room ready to change for her VIP.

Chapter 3

Monica

"I don't give a fuck how longs it takes! Imma find that bitch, Shasta Smithson, and that hoe gone get the business for my Big!" Monica said as she hit her fist against the table in her shit hole piece of an apartment.

Tears start to roll down Monica's face, as she studies the picture of her and Big in Tahiti celebrating their honeymoon. Since Big's death in Miami, Monica's lifestyle had taken a dramatic, stressful change; a full 360 in other words. She went from a three bedroom condo in Buckhead to a one bedroom apartment in the center of the Bluff off Lindsey Street; dead center of the trap. She had to sell her jewelry to bury Big because he had no life insurance. The only thing she got left of value is all of her expensive ass clothes Big bought her. If it wasn't for her ex-manager from when she used to work at the Mexican Bar, who gave her, her job back with no questions asked. She'd be super fucked up right now.

"This is not my fucking life!" yelled Monica.

"I'm gone get that bitch. I promise to fucking life, Imma get dat bitch if I don't do nothing else!"

Monica wiped the tears from her face and jumped back into beast mode. She pulled out her laptop and started scrolling through her

Lynise

emails, hoping that cybercam1908 had finally found the information she had been searching for, for months.

He did.

"Thank you! It's about fucking time," Monica said, reading cyberccam1908's email.

It read:

Didn't I tell you I was a genius? I found your Ms. Shasta Smithson as requested. However, before I share anything, I'm going to need that $600 transferred to my account.

RTE# 066.192.555

ACCT# 00691863400

Once the funds post, I will email you the rest of the information you desire. Yours truly, cybercam1908.

"Now that's what I'm talking about!" said Monica, still talking to herself--happy as fuck like she just hit the Powerball or something.

Pacing through her apartment, Monica stopped and took a deep breath, then she grabbed her purse to retrieve her pre-paid Rush card. She had exactly $6,473.32 to her name. These last eight months all she did was work hard, chat online with cybercam1908, and think about how she was going to make Shasta pay for fucking up her life.

"Bitch, I'm coming!"

"I'm coming and you won't even see me coming." She grinned.

Monica quickly transferred the money, emailed cybercam1908 the confirmation receipt, and sat desperately by her laptop awaiting cybercam's response.

Several minutes later, cybercam1908 responded to her email.

It read:

The Shasta Smithson you been looking for is now known as Shasta Davis. She relocated a year ago from Atlanta to Essex, CT. Her address is 25 Hemlock Dr. 06426. Even better...wait for it... wait for it...just playing! She's also a very successful club owner. She was featured in last month's CT's New Rise To Power Magazine for having one of the top gentlemen's club up north has seen in a while

TWO TIMES BETRAYED

by the name of Luxury. The website is shastaluxury.com, on there you will find other contact information such as her number. Wait a minute, I have that for you too. (203) 555-6716. Your welcome and you know how to reach me if you need anything else.

Yours truly,
Cybercam1908

"Now that's what the fuck I'm talking 'bout!" Monica danced around her laptop.

"Let me calm my ass down," breathing heavily, she had to catch her breath.

Singing to herself, "Imma get you bitch, Imma get you bitch," Monica pulled her laptop back out and emailed cybercam a thank you. Then she sat down and typed in Shasta's web address to take a look at what she'd been up to for herself. Immediately, as she scrolled through the site, Monica's heart began to fill with hate.

"Oh, so this bitch been living it up off my fucking money! I'm stuck down here in this piece of shit apartment with tile for carpet, a kitchen the size of a fucking closet, and a damn fan for A/C!"

Suddenly a light bulb set off in Monica's head as she continued to read through the website she came across a huge advertisement that read:

ALWAYS HIRING NEW ENTERTAINERS, UNLIMITED INCOME.

That was Monica's way into Shasta's world. Although they had only met once before at the club she and Kila used to dance at, she still thought that it would be wise for her to change her name and shit just to be on the safe side. You never know what could trigger someone's memory, on top of all the pictures her and Big took at the club for Black's birthday party. She didn't wanna take any chances. Not this soon in the game.

"Anyway better safe than sorry," Monica said, still talking to her laptop. Outside of her manager Kelly and Cybercam1908, she had very few people she would confide in. Especially now.

Monica emailed cybercam1908.

Lynise

It read:

I've been thinking it's time I too relocate. Is it possible that you can get me a new identity? I got a $1,000 for it and I need it ASAP! Get @ me soon as you get this.

Till then,

Monica

She quickly closed her laptop, rolled up the last of the Loud she had and got ready for work. Monica had a new glow about herself. She felt ever more confident and relieved that she was now finally closer to getting her revenge on the person who she felt ruined her life.

Chapter 4

Sending For The Wolf

B*eep! Beep! Beep!*
Shasta tossed and turned, still half asleep and searching for her alarm clock.
Beep! Beep! Beep!
"Fuck, I hate Monday's!" yelled Shasta, irritated at the sound of her alarm clock going off for the second time in five minutes. Still sounding, she reached over and threw it off the nightstand.
"I'm up! I'm up. Damn."
Lil' Chris runs into her room.
"Mommy? Are you fighting with the clock again?" asked Lil' Chris.
Shasta yawned.
"And you know it, baby," she replied. Her son snickered at her.
"I've already lost count on how many clocks you buy every week," her son said.
Shasta got of bed and tackled her son back down to the bed with her.
"Funny. You got jokes?" she said, still tickling her son on her bed.
"If only I had the energy you had, I wouldn't need an alarm clock," Shasta replied as she kissed Lil' Chris repeatedly all over his face.

Lynise

"Mama!" said her son acting shy. She wiped the kisses off as she plants them on his face.

"What…you too big to want my kisses?" Shasta asked.

"No, it's not that."

"Then what is it?"

"You still have morning breath!" replied Lil' Chris as he ran to the other side of the room.

"Cooties," he said, crossing his fingers behind his back.

Shasta just stood there for a second, smiling.

"I'll show you cooties," she replied running toward her son.

"Okay, okay you won!" her son laughed hysterically.

"I always do," gesturing for Lil' Chris hand to get him to calm down for a second.

"Anyway baby, when you get out of school today I need for you to go chill with Ryan and Zack. I got some errands to run so I won't be here when you come home."

Lil' Chris big bright smile turned upside down. Shasta grabbed his face to look at her and not the floor.

"I promise I'll be here before you go to bed."

Lil' Chris was still upset.

"Aww, baby, don't be that way. Don't you remember the plan? Our vision?" she asked her son.

"Yes, ma'am."

"And what is it?"

"You have to work long nights in order to make good money, so that we can have work free days in the future." Said Lil' Chris as she recited along with him.

"That's right. We will be where we need to be real soon; then we can move back to Atlanta. Scratch that, move closer to Atlanta so we can visit Grandma, Auntie Candy and Auntie Nancy."

"I know I just wish the future was today."

"You know you are extremely too smart to be only six." Shasta said as she picked up her son and kissed him on the forehead sitting him down on her lap.

"I know. What can I say? I'm a genius," her son smiled from ear to ear.

"Yes, you are my little genius."

"Now gone get your clothes on Ryan & Zack will be here in a minute."

"Okay. I love you Mommy."

"I love you more."

Moments later, Shasta heard Ryan & Zack ringing the doorbell for Lil' Chris.

"You boys have a good day at school and don't get into no trouble."

Lil' Chris blew her a kiss and took off running with his friends in direction of the bus stop. Watching as the boys quickly disappeared off to school; she picked up the toys off the front porch and went back inside the house.

"I might as well stay up." Shasta said out loud to herself, throwing the toys in the hamper Lil' Chris keeps in the living room. She heads to the kitchen to prepare her daily mojo juice which consisted of one part Columbian coffee and one-part American five-hour energy. While that's brewing, Shasta runs upstairs to grab her cell phone off the night stand and her laptop from out of Lil' Chris's room.

"Imma have to buy my baby his own laptop. He stay hijacking mine."

Back in the kitchen, while sipping her mojo juice, Shasta checks the employment requests off her Luxury page. With her always hiring and firing, Shasta needed at least three more dancers to cover Yung Fresh "I'm 'bout dat" single release party.

I really need to give Stacey more responsibility, she thought to herself.

Scrolling through hundreds of girls who would give their first born just to work a shift at Luxury, Shasta narrowed her search down to five. Amongst the five she came across, Valerie Alexis Carter's profile.

"Damn, this bitch bad as fuck. She most definitely gotta come be a part of what Club Luxury got going on."

Shasta continued to read, then emailed Valerie offering her and invitation to come up north to interview personally for Club Luxury.

It read:

After reviewing your profile, I feel you would be a good candidate to join Club Luxury. I deal with only high-end clients and if you're anything like your profile in person, I'm for sure my clients would love you—lots of money to be made. RSVP and I'll have a plane ticket waiting for you at the airport. I need confirmation by noon EST time.

Hope to see you soon,
Shasta

Once the email was sent to Valerie, Shasta sat for a few more minutes deleting the spam mail and useless solicitations. Right before she was about to logout her Luxury account, she saw a response from Valerie. It just so happen to be the quickest response ever. Yet she paid it no mind, she was glad Valerie responded as fast as she did. She wanted her at her club.

It read:

Thank you for the opportunity and I look forward to meeting with you. This ol' Louisiana country girl can't wait to come up North and make some real money. You can send my plane ticket for pick up at Louis Armstrong International Airport.

See you soon,
Valerie

Shasta grabs her cell and calls her travel agent. Her agent, Dallas, picks up on the first ring.

"Who you flying up this time?" Dallas said, assuming he already knew what the call was about.

"So you a fucking physic now?" laughed Shasta.

"Naw, I just know you're always working, and since you've been a client of mine, you've never once called for yourself," replied Dallas.

"I promise I will one day. Anyway I need a flight out Louisiana to here."

"Coach or First Class?" Dallas asked.

Shasta went back to Valerie's picture to determine her flight value, although she thought she was bad, First Class is First Class. It was her money she was spending.

"First Class," said Shasta

"She must be a good one," replied Dallas in his most feminine voice.

"Ha. Does it matter? Ain't like you gone be trying to smash her!"

"Ewww...damn skippy. I hate y'all sluts. I'll take a nice, strong muscular man that will bend me over and..." before Dallas could finish his statement, Shasta cut him off.

"Dallas! My ears! I bet you will, but I don't wanna hear dat shit!" Said Shasta

"Mmm, huh. Neway bitch, how soon you need this damn ticket? And will this be one way or round trip?"

"Make it one way, and for tomorrow morning. If the bitch don't look nothing like her profile, she gone be finding her own way back to da 504!

"I hear that."

Shasta heard Dallas click a few more buttons, seconds later the flight confirmation was in her email.

"You got it?" asked Dallas.

"Yeah, doll," replied Shasta.

"Well minority, it was a pleasure. I do have clients that's more important than you, so I gotta end this," said Dallas, jokingly as usual.

"Whatever! You know there's now one more important than me. That's' why you stay picking up on the first ring," responded Shasta.

"Yeah, yeah. Imma let you have that one."

"Uh, huh, I know you will."

"Bye, slut!"

"Bye, I hate that I'm not a real woman!"

They laughed and hung up the phone. Shasta then emailed Valerie her flight itinerary and directions to the club.

G STREET CHRONICLES
A LITERARY POWERHOUSE
WWW.GSTREETCHRONICLES.COM

Chapter 5

Carmen

Loud sounds of the move and drop of furniture, along with the sounds of shattered glass, Nico drags Carmen by the hair from the living room to the balcony. Carmen screams as Nico repeatedly punches her in the face.

"What I do? What I do?" cries Carmen.

"Shut the fuck up! Bitch shut the fuck up!" replies Nico as he punches Carmen in the face again.

"This time you finna miss work bitch!"

Nico took a quick second off Carmen's ass to hit da sack of cocaine he had and grabbed the flower pot. Nico took the flower pot and bashed Carmen across the head with it. All you heard was screams of agony coming from Carmen, with no one to help and not a phone in sight she was fucked up. What else could she do but take it. She damn sure was too weak at this point to even attempt to fight back. Blacking out as she often did, she went numb. Thinking to herself, *he's going to kill me one day.* Each time the beatings got worse and worse. Thinking how he's the one that constantly cheats and lies and how she's the one beat as if it was her fucking up.

Nico throws the last punch that his energy can muster up before he locks Carmen outside on the balcony.

"You fucking bitch! Stay yo' ass out here for a while. That will

Lynise

teach you bitch not to play with me!" ranted Nico.

Ms. Caroline observes the abuse from her balcony across the street, as bad as she wants to call the police. She knows ain't no use. Carmen would only deny the assault as she has done many times before. Nico sees Ms. Caroline looking and shoots a bird at her. Ms. Caroline shoots one back. Leaving Carmen on the balcony, Nico leaves for work as if he ain't did shit.

Face bloody. Carmen lay on the balcony badly beaten. The only thing she was able to do was cry. Her eyes swollen to the point she could barely see, she passes out just to awaken hours later on Ms. Caroline's couch. Carmen didn't realize how bad her face looked until she saw the tears start to form in Ms. Caroline's eyes.

"Ahhhh." said Carmen in pain from the ice pack Ms. Caroline was putting on her face. Barely able to move, Carmen allowed for Ms. Caroline to gently replace the ice pack back onto her face.

"Baby girl, I don't know for the life of me why you just won't leave him. Suga don't you know he's going to kill you one day," said Ms. Caroline as tears started to roll down her cheek.

"I'm okay, I'm okay," said Carmen. You could hear the sadness in her response.

"No you're not. No you're fucking not!"

"What type of man beats a woman?" asked Ms. Caroline angrily.

"He's just really stressed out Ms. Caroline, with his job, and with me working at the club. He be worrying about all the niggas who in my face every night. Don't worry about me, Imma be okay."

"I'm sorry Carmen, but that ain't no fucking excuse! I let Mark daddy beat me for eight long years before I got up enough nerve to leave him. You don't wanna get to the point of it being you or him, and that's where I was. He's going to hurt you real bad, baby girl."

"Please don't continue to let him use you as his punching bag. It's only going to get worse," said Ms. Caroline with pain in her heart for Carmen as if she was her own daughter.

Carmen laid in Ms. Caroline's arms and just broke down crying.

TWO TIMES BETRAYED

"I don't know how to leave him, he's all I got and all I know," cried Carmen.

Ms. Caroline just holds her and rocks her back and forth, trying to hold back the tears of her own that won't seem to stop following.

"I don't have anybody else," cries Carmen profusely.

"You got me."

"You got me," replied Ms. Caroline.

Ms. Caroline wipes the tears from Carmen's eyes and continued to hold her as she started to fall back asleep.

"Everything is going to be okay," said Ms. Caroline, running her hand across Carmen's hair in a motherly nature.

Ms. Caroline hurriedly slid up from under Carmen once she saw that Carmen had falling back asleep for sure. Being as quiet as she could, Ms. Caroline rushed to the kitchen for her phone.

"This is the last fucking time dat punk pussy bitch gone beat on her!" said Ms. Caroline, heated now and mad as fuck after the emotional shit.

Ms. Caroline dials her son Mark. He picks up on the first ring.

"Momma, what's wrong?" asked Mark.

"It's Carmen."

Mark got outta bed, and went into his bathroom.

"He hit her again, didn't he?"

"Yeah, and it's much worse this time. He gone fuck around and kill her, Mark."

"Say no more. Where is she?"

"She's in there on the couch asleep. I just got her to calm down about thirty minutes ago."

"I'm on my way."

"Ok."

Mark always had love for Carmen, not the relationship kind… more like the brother and sister kind. They grew up together in Perry Holmes and their mothers were best friends. When Carmen's mother died ten years ago, Ms. Caroline stepped in and raised Carmen; she

Lynise

lived with her till she turned twenty-three and started working for Shasta, by that time Mark had been moved out. Carmen's mother is who convinced Caroline to move up North, in order to get away from Mark's daddy.

A couple hours later, Mark was beating on his mother's front door.

"Why you ain't use your key?" asked Ms. Caroline, signaling to Mark to quiet down because she didn't want to wake Carmen.

"I left it. I just jumped in the car and came straight over here," said Mark as he hugged his mother. He could see Carmen lying on the couch. Fighting back tears of his own he just stared at her, noticing how swoll and fucked up her face was.

See the history. Mark and Shasta ran in the same circle back in Atlanta. He was a big time street Pharmacist who supplied most of the niggas who used to frequent the club she and Kila danced at. He was also known in the streets as a hit man; which was his true talent. When Shasta relocated to Connecticut, she ran into Carmen at a grocery store not long after she closed her deal to open up Luxury. Matter of fact, Carmen was her first employee. Shasta found out Mark lived in Connecticut because he had dropped Carmen off at the club a few times before Carmen bought her car. They both treated Carmen like a lil sister and both felt the need to protect her. Now on the other hand, Nico was originally from Detroit. He met Carmen at Luxury. He used to come in every night just to see if she was working. For three months straight, he was trying to get Carmen's attention. Of course, Carmen eventually gave in to Nico's charm; they began dating and it was good for about six months. After that, Nico started showing his true colors just as sho' as night meets day; and it's been hell for her ever since. That was two years ago.

Body aching, Carmen manages to pull herself upward on the couch after she hears Mark's voice.

"Yo' momma called you to my rescue again?" said Carmen, trying to minimize her fucked-up situation.

Ms. Caroline sat at the end of the couch by her, brushing the hair

TWO TIMES BETRAYED

out of her face as she spoke to Mark.

"Captain America, boo. You know Imma be here every time," replied Mark.

"And how does Tina feel about you leaving her side at 4:00 in the morning?" asked Carmen, barely getting her words out.

"You ain't gotta worry 'bout dat…you family."

Carmen nodded.

"Look at you. Why you keep letting that nigga beat you like that? What the fuck is wrong with you, shawty? Look at your face, shawty!" Mark said, mad as fuck.

"I'm good, brah; we just had a little scuffle that's all."

"Lil scuffle my ass! He's gone kill her Mark," said Ms. Caroline.

"No, fuck he ain't. This the last time I'm finna see you looking like this, shawty. For real, for real. I got something for that fuck nigga. Bet dat!" Mark said, staring Carmen dead in her eyes.

"I said, I'm good!" yelled Carmen.

"I know and Imma make sure that's ah true statement shawty."

Carmen grabs Ms. Caroline's cell to call Shasta. Shasta picks up, knowing something's up.

"What up?" asked Shasta.

Carmen takes a deep breath.

"Imma have to be off tonight," said Carmen, feeling a little embarrassed.

"Let me guess…Nico beat you up again?"

"Yes," replied Carmen.

"Imma call you back. I'm calling Mark this shit gotta stop!" said Shasta getting madder by the second.

"You ain't gotta do that. I'm at Ms. Caroline house and he's already over here."

"Well, put him on the fucking phone!" demanded Shasta.

Carmen handed Mark the phone.

"What up Sis?"

"Is it bad, brah?" asked Shasta.

Lynise

"Hell, yeah, sis. She fucked up. She won't be in for at least a week."

Shasta leaves her room to continue her conversation, she had let Lil' Chris sleep in her room last night, and she ain't wanna wake him this early.

"Mark, you gotta do something 'bout that fuck nigga. She ain't strong enough to leave him. He gone fuck around and kill her. We can't let that happen, brah."

"I know. I got that nigga for real for real. Y'all ain't gotta stress, Imma take care of it."

"Okay, cool. Let me know if you need ANYTHING! Tell Carmen Imma come by and see her later."

"I will."

"Lata," said Shasta.

"Lata," replied Mark as they both hung up the phone.

Carmen crawled back up into the fetal position. She knew in her heart that one day soon would be the last time she would see Nico alive. She also knew that if she kept allowing Nico to beat on her, he would eventually end up killing her; the thought of her dying at his hands sadden her. Although she loved Nico, she ain't wanna go out like that. She knew she had to step back and let Mark do what he knows best. Feeling guilty 'bout her thoughts, she just laid there emotionless. Mark and Ms. Caroline watched her closely as she fell back asleep.

Chapter 6

New Identity

"Fuck! I'm getting real impatient, cybercam1908," yelled Monica as she sat outside still sitting in her car in front of her apartment.

"What the hell is taking him so fucking long to get me my shit?"

Monica laid her head against her steering wheel, dreading to go in her closet size of an apartment. Her neighbors by now were used to seeing her fight with the dash board each night before getting out the car. Unwillingly, she finally got out and headed straight for her door. Monica never mixed or mingled with her neighbors. It was only hi and bye with her; unfortunately, this time she had no choice before she could get her key in good. Her neighbor walked over.

"Is yo' name Monica Reed?" asked the neighbor.

Looking at the lady with a puzzled face, Moncia took the key out the door and focused her attention to her neighbor.

"Yeah. Why?" asked Monica.

"Then wait a second before you take it in. I gotta package over my house that came for you today. My husband said he signed for it," replied the neighbor, leaving to go get her mail.

"Why in the fuck would her husband sign for my shit?" mumbled Monica.

Curious and irritated, Monica waited. She had no idea what it was, and the only mail she every got was bills.

"If this lady on some fuck shit, I swear..." said Monica, getting even more irritated at this point.

Her neighbor came back out her apartment minutes later holding a FedEx envelope in her hand. She handed the envelope over to Monica and stood there hoping that Monica was going to open the mail up front of her curious to see what it was also. Mainly because when her husband signed for the envelope, she couldn't tell what it was without making it obvious that they had already tampered with her shit. Monica wasn't stupid; she could already tell they had already been trying to go in her shit—she ain't say nothing though.

"Da FedEx man brought it to my door, so we just held it for you," said the neighbor like she was doing Monica a favor.

"Thank you," replied Monica.

Still standing there, Moncia couldn't help but notice the neighbor's facial expression. She reached in her purse and took out a $20 bill and gave it to the lady. Grabbing the money, the lady's eyes never met with Monica's; for sure if they had, she would have seen in Monica's face how irritated she really was with her.

That's all she wanted was a reward for getting someone else's mail that she had no business signing for in the first damn place, Monica thought.

"Thank you, thank you; but you ain't have to do that. We neighbors, we gotta look out for each other," said the lady.

"Uh, huh, we sure do," said Monica, brushing her neighbor off as she opened her door.

Monica quickly went inside to avoid further conversation with her neighbor. She shook the envelope but she still had no clue on what was inside. She threw her purse on the couch and ripped the mail open. The contents of the envelope fell on the floor. Monica's eyes widened with excitement. It was her new identity she had been waiting on for weeks now. Louisiana driver's license and social security card along with a letter from cybercam1908.

TWO TIMES BETRAYED

It read:

Yeah, I know you thought I forgot about. Well, I didn't. It just took a little longer than I anticipated; anyway, you have it now. Let me know if you need anything else.

Genius truly,

Cybercam1908

P.S. send my cash soon as you get this. I'd hate to register your new identity as FBI's Most Wanted List for non-payment of services. Not a good look.

Monica sat on the couch with one of the largest evil grin she could ever imagine. Nothing but hate motivated her at this point.

"Valerie Alexis Carter," said Monica, staring at the driver's license and social security card.

"How the fuck he get a picture of me though. I damn sho' don't remember sending him one; but, oh well, I don't care," she said, talking to herself.

Monica pulled out her laptop and wired cybercam1908 his money along with a thank you letter. Twenty minutes later, her shit was packed and in her car, headed to New Orleans, Louisiana to stay with her cousin Arie a few weeks while she put the second half of her plan into motion.

"Bitch, I'm on my way," said Monica.

All she took were a few pairs of clothes and the pictures she had of her and Big. She honked the horn to get her neighbor's attention. The lady came outside. Monica handed her the keys to her apartment and told her to help herself.

Lindsey Street in her rearview mirror, the motivation of revenge surged through her veins like poison. Monica Nicole Reed was now Valerie Alexis Carter, and the only thing she cared about was getting her revenge. Her only thoughts were to get Shasta for ruining her life as she so truly believed she had.

G STREET CHRONICLES
A LITERARY POWERHOUSE
WWW.GSTREETCHRONICLES.COM

Chapter 7

The Asset

Two months had quickly passed by since Valerie had first started working for Shasta's club, Luxury. For a woman who's never danced before outside of the private dances she would do for Big, Valerie was really making a name for herself. She was bringing in a lot of wealthy clients from all over—clients who flew in and waited hours just to see her. Of course, Shasta was impressed by the numbers Valerie was doing. So much impressed, that when new money entered the club, she was the first to be presented to accompany the gentlemen inside the "Fun Room" outside of Maui.

Shasta also started inviting Valerie to events outside the club that didn't require you to take your clothes off. Shasta would have her escorting clients from the airport to the club, sending her on dinner dates with clients, hosting parties with her. Shasta even had her come to a few charity events she was sponsoring down in South Philly.

Indeed, Monica's end game was quickly coming into effect. All she needed was Shasta's trust, which she was slowing earning with every check Shasta cashed on her behalf. Valerie was becoming ever more confident that she was getting closer to getting the revenge she felt she deserved for Big's sake.

Sitting alone in her living room, Monica picked up the picture she had of her and Big off the table and rubbed her hand across his face.

Lynise

"Baby, we almost home," Monica said, talking to the picture.

"I'm slowly reeling that bitch in; by the time she realize what's going on, it's gone be too fucking late."

Monica's venting was interrupted by the vibrations of her phone. She had three missed calls.

"Speaking of the bitch, this is her now," said Monica, still talking to Big's picture. She kissed it then placed it back on the stand next to the couch where she was sitting.

Monica noticed that all three missed calls were from Shasta, so she let her go to voicemail again.

"I ain't answering for that bitch."

"If it's important, she will call back."

"I'm an asset now; plus, that bitch knows I've gotten other offers to dance out of clubs in Vegas and LA. She's doing whatever to keep me on a leash. I got that bitch right where I want her," said Monica with a new-found arrogance in her tone.

"She will be calling back in 5, 4, 3, 2..." before she got to one, Shasta was ringing her line again.

Valerie picked up this time.

"What's up lady, I been blowing you up. You forget I'm the boss?" asked Shasta.

"My bad sweetie, I was in the shower. What's up with ya?" replied Valerie.

"Same ol', getting this money. I was calling because I have a big-time investor flying in this evening. I'm thinking 'bout opening up a Luxury Phase 2 on the Southside and I could use his check.

"Okay. So what you need for me to do?" asked Valerie.

"I want you at the meeting. You might remember him, he's been to the club a few times, but anyway, he been hearing 'bout you and he wanna meet you before we even begin to talk numbers."

"Damn, really?"

"Yeah, really."

Valerie giggled in admiration of herself. Shasta laughed as well still in awe about the conditions of the meeting.

"What the fuck you doing to them niggas in the "Fun Room" to where they can't make a business decision without pussy in they face?" asked Shasta jokingly.

Valerie quietly jumped up and down in the middle of her living room, thinking to herself that this was just what she needed to hook Shasta.

"I'll never tell."

"So anyway, Imma need you to meet at the club, let's say 7:00 p.m. You can ride with me; the meeting gone be at The Four Seasons. Y'all meet, talk, eat, fuck or do whatever. I just need him on board when it comes time to talk this money. I'm talking BIG money. I know you 'bout that life, right?"

"Hell, yeah, I am. Imma be there—dressed to impress," replied Valerie.

"Shit, go right, you gone be taken care of for the rest of your life. I'm talking just that much money."

"Damn, for real?"

"Yeah, for real for real; so bitch, you betta make me look good."

"I got you, I'll be there at 7:00 p.m."

"Aiight, see you in a few, hun."

"Okay," said Valerie. They both hung up.

Barely being able to keep her composure while on the phone with Shasta, Monica picked Big's picture back up and started talking to it again.

"I'm reeling this bitch right on in baby."

"She has no clue who she fucking wit," said Monica more motivated that ever.

Monica ran up the stairs in her new condo she leased a month ago. She went straight to the closet to pull out her brand new Gucci black pants suit tailor-made only for her, along with the matching handbag and pumps. Dressed in all black, she was on her 007 shit, ready to complete the mission.

G STREET CHRONICLES
A LITERARY POWERHOUSE
WWW.GSTREETCHRONICLES.COM

Chapter 8

I Run This Shit

"Damn. I'm tired as fuck!" said Shasta turning on the lamp, once again throwing her alarm clock off the night stand. "I swear I'm finna start home schooling Lil' Chris."

Shasta rolled and tapped the nigga she brought home last night. Moaning in irritation, he turned over the opposite direction.

"Fuck! He was supposed to be gone."

Shasta picked up her cell phone to double check what time it was again, upset cause now she only had thirty minutes to get Lil' Chris ready for school.

"Nigga, get yo' ass up. It's time to for you to go!" demanded Shasta.

"Damn, girl you tripping," he replied.

"Man nigga, get yo' ass up, get dressed and leave out the back. My son will be running in here any minute."

"Come on now. You know what the move is. Do we really gotta go through this shit every time we fuck?" asked Shasta as she snatched the covers off Smash In, whose name was really Jackson; she just liked calling him Smash In for some reason. He hated it, but she ain't care.

"Naw, hell naw," said Smash In as he sat up and got out of bed wiping his eyes looking for his boxers and shit.

Shasta now fully awake had his pants in her hands standing at the

Lynise

door feeling like she done committed the ultimate sin…only because he was married.

"It was fun, bae," Shasta smiled.

"You finna stop using me for my dick shawty; for real."

"Ahh. Don't be so emotional. You know you like when I use you," replied Shasta walking toward him and handing him his pants. Smash In tried to grab her by the waist, but Shasta pulled away.

"I'll call you. Now hurry yo' ass up before my son walk in here."

Smash In just looked at her.

"You know you the only bitch that make me feel cheap after I fuck," said Smash In, putting his last shoe on.

"Yeah, yeah. It's impossible for you to feel cheap. Especially when your ass worth almost 100 million dollars. Get the fuck outa here with that shit. I ain't going for that. Nigga, stop trippin' and speed it up, you know you will be back," said Shasta, holding her bedroom door open for him.

Smash In walked toward her. He reached over and kissed her on the cheek, then whispered in her ear, trying to sound seductive.

"My wife knows about us now, boo; which is starting to take the fun outta the whole sneaking around thing. You need to follow suit before it's too late.

Shasta backed up face up and sucked her teeth like whatever.

"First of all honey, I follow no one, they follow me. Secondly, I could give two fucks 'bout your whore of a wife finding out about us."

"Hell, her name should be Smash In too! Two of a fucking kind."

She could tell she was getting to him by the last comment she made. He tried to hide it like her words didn't matter. Standing in the door way with his clothes half on and the other half in his hands, he just starred at her.

"Ha, ha. You got jokes now. It's cool. You will need me for something, just watch and see. I see straight through the guards and Visas as much as you pretend not to care. I know you do," said Smash In.

TWO TIMES BETRAYED

He reached over and tried to kiss her again. This time she put her hand up to block it. "It's like that?" asked Smash In.

"Whatever," replied Shasta, walking Smash In out her room to the garage.

"It's like that shawty?" he asked again.

"You will be alright."

Shasta stood and watched as he got in his car waiting for him to pull off. Smash In honked the horn as he pulled off, right when Shasta thought he was good out her driveway. He put his Benz in reverse, pulled back in her driveway with his windows rolled down playing, "If you think you're lonely now" loud enough for her neighbors to hear it while he sang along. Shasta stood there and just laughed.

"This fool need help, Imma have to stop fucking with his crazy ass," she said to herself.

Smash In sped off. Shasta turned around and went in the house with the garage door closing behind her this time. She didn't want another episode of him putting his car in reverse again playing something else, she didn't want to hear.

Shasta made her way to her kitchen to make her daily mojo juice. Smiling at how she be handling these niggas. She took great satisfaction in sending them niggas home, she started to reflect on how her and Kila would get put out the hotel room after niggas got what they wanted from them. Now she putting niggas out and she loved the feeling—the feeling of being in control.

"Dat nigga think just cause he gotta check, I'm pose to cling to his ass like some kinda fucking puppy. Shitting'me? I got my own check, anyway he flexin'. Dat nigga ain't finna stop fucking with me. Soon as call his ass and tell I'm trying to fuck. He gone be on his way," said Shasta, talking to herself while she checked her missed messages and emails.

Shasta sat at the kitchen table just thinking of all she had to do today. She had a full fifteen minutes of me time before she had to get Lil' Chris up. Still floating off the successful meeting she had with

Lynise

Valerie and her new investor a few days back. Shasta couldn't wait to start looking for a new property for Luxury Phase 2.

"This shit is so surreal," said Shasta as she turned on her Boze surround sound beating the only CD she kept in there. Young Jeezy. Singing along to her favorite pep me up song...*Listen up, I got some child support fa'ya. Get off yo' ass bitch, get you a job.*

Rolling her a blunt of Loud, Shasta continue vibin real hard to "I'm back" turning the music up louder and louder. If Lil' Chris wasn't up, he was sure to be up now.

"I swear Jeezy stay going in. He always speak da truth," said Shasta as she replayed her favorite song for the third time now.

"I gotta get him to come to my club, ASAP," Shasta said, feeling real motivated.

Shasta grabbed her mojo and followed the music to the living room in search of her purse.

"He gotta come to my 4th of July Completely Naked International Bash this year. Damn, I love that man!"

Pacing her living room floor, jamming…she was so turnt up, she ain't even notice that Lil' Chris had already got up and gotten dressed. He was sitting on the couch just watching and listening to her talk to herself as he has caught doing many times before. When he finally did speak, he scared the shit outa her.

"Mommy," yelled Lil' Chris, trying to speak over the music.

Shasta jumped and then danced her way over towards him, turning the music down so she could rap with son.

"Damn, baby you scared me. How long you been sitting there?" asked Shasta.

"Umm, since damn I love that man," Lil' Chris repeated.

"Ha, ha," said Shasta as she reached over to hug her son.

"What I tell you 'bout sneaking up on me?"

"How I sneak in my own house," yawned Lil' Chris.

Shasta hugged him even tighter.

"You're too smart for your age."

"I know ma. You tell me that all the time."

Shasta kissed Lil' Chris on his forehead.

"What I can't compliment my most important man?" asked Shasta tickling her son and playfully poking him on his sides.

Laughter comes loudly from Lil' Chris's mouth.

"I like compliments," said Lil' Chris still laughing.

Shasta leaned down and kissed him on the forehead again.

"It's about that time for you to leave for school."

"Ugh...I know, another day of me teaching them something," said Lil' Chris as if his mother's last statement had sucked the fun out the room.

Lil' Chris dragged his feet as he left to go upstairs and get his book bag.

"Well my love, it's Friday, you ain't gotta worry about getting up early and teaching anyone anything tomorrow."

"Ahh, I still don't wanna go."

"Well you have to. It ah be over before you know it."

"You will be alright."

Lil' Chris still standing on the steps, "Ain't that what you just told Smash In?" asked Lil' Chris.

Shasta liked to have dropped her mojo. Shocked at what her son just said, she would have never knew that all the time she had been fucking with Smash In, Lil' Chris knew 'bout it.

"Boy, get yo ass up them steps and go get your book bag," she replied, making her way closer to the steps to where he was. Lil' Chris laughs and takes off running up the steps. Shasta couldn't do nothing but smile. She tried to hit him with a pillow she grabbed of the couch, but she missed.

"Whatever, Lil boy! Imma get you. You gotta come back down here," Shasta laughed.

Shaking her head, she made her way back to the kitchen to refill her mojo. A few moments later, Lil' Chris was running into the kitchen to get his lunch. Shasta kissed him goodbye and watched as he ran out

Lynise

to meet Ryan and Zack at the bus stop.

Turning her music back up, Shasta grabs her cell and sees she has three messages from Smash In.

Msg 1: I miss you

Msg 2: I wanna see you tonight

Msg 3: I love you ;)

What the fuck. He trippin', she thought to herself as she erased them all.

Chapter 9

Stacey & Mr. Delowe.

Shasta got to the club today early than usual. Normally it was Stacey who was there first. She was excited about the second meeting she was going to have with the investor this morning. They were finally going to sit down and go over the details for the grand opening of Luxury Phase 2.

"Damn."

"Who died?" asked Stacey jokingly.

"No one," laughed Shasta.

"I'm just saying though, I ain't never seen you here this early since we opened up two years ago," replied Stacey.

"I know right."

"What's the occasion for you to be gracing me with your presence?" asked Stacey.

"Well, I have a meeting with Mark Delowe in a few hours, and I wanted to talk to you 'bout something."

"Um. Okay. About what?" asked Stacey with concern in her voice.

"Relax girl. It's good, honey."

"Whoa. 'Cause I'm straight on fucked-up news for this week," replied Stacey

"Is everything okay? What's kinda of fucked up news you got this week?" asked Shasta.

Lynise

"You know. Carmen. I just hate that she going through that shit. She is way too young and pretty to be letting some muthafucka pound on her," said Stacey.

"Say no more. Mark taking care of that as we speak. She won't have to worry about that nigga soon," said Shasta as she walked to the bar to pour her a glass of champagne.

"Girl, I can't wait to piss on his grave." Replied Stacey

"You ain't the only."

"You want a glass of champagne?" asked Shasta

"Yeah sure, It's five o'clock somewhere," laughed Stacey

They both toasted there glasses up.

"To more money than we both can spend," said Stacey.

"Bet."

"Now, let's get to business."

"Okay, what's on your mind?" asked Stacey as she took a seat at the bar.

"As you know, Luxury Phase 2 will be opening soon."

"That I do," replied Stacey.

"Well, you've been good to me here. You keep this place running and making stupid money when I'm away."

Stacey nodded in agreement.

"Basically what I'm getting at is that I want you to start taking on more responsibility."

"So far, I've grown to trust you. I need for you to be my right hand now," said Shasta.

"Really, Shasta?" asked Stacey with a huge ass smile on her face.

"Really."

"Imma need you more than ever these next few months. It's gone be some long hours, at least until we bring on extra trustworthy staff. Which is gone be your job as well."

"Matter of fact, if you accept this promotion, Imma need you to hire at least 100 new girls before the grand opening."

"I got you. I'm ready and I'm honored you chose me Shasta."

TWO TIMES BETRAYED

"Stacey girl, you were my only choice," said Shasta reaching in her handbag for the already prepared check she had for Stacey. Shasta came from behind the bar and handed Stacey the envelope.

Stacey opened the envelope and couldn't believe what she saw. Shasta had given her a check for $250,000. Stacey started to cry immediately, and hugged Shasta tightly.

"It's okay girl. You most definitely deserve it," said Shasta, still hugging Stacey.

"Thank you. Thank you, I want let you down. I swear," said Stacey, wiping the tears from her eyes.

"I know, now past me a napkin. Yo' ass got tears all over my damn Armani."

"Whoa! Whoa!" yelled Stacey, passing Shasta a napkin from the bar; excited and happy as ever.

"Now you can get rid of that God awful cheap ass car!" laughed Shasta.

"I can't wait to get rid of that car girl."

"Matter of fact, go do that now. I want you back here riding clean before Mr. Delowe gets here. I can't have my right hand in a hooptie meeting the man."

Jumping up and down in happiness, Stacey ran off to her office, grabbed her handbag and headed for the car lot.

"Something new, Benz, Lexus, or Jag!" yelled Shasta.

"Okay!" Stacey yelled back.

Shasta went back behind the bar and poured her another glass of champagne.

"That went well." Shasta out loud.

Feeling real proud that she was finally in a position to help out someone she cared about other than family. Shit, Stacey was family now. A quarter million dollars' worth of it.

A couple hours later Mr. Delowe was pulling up in front of the club.

While Stacey was gone, Shasta took upon herself to prepare a nice

Lynise

little setting for Mr. Delowe's arrival. In her office she had an elegant gold and diamond serving tray Jackson, aka Smash In, bought her last year from Paris. The tray was full of the biggest, juiciest strawberries imported from Beijing's Wander Gardern, imported Bitto cheese, and the very expensive Krug Brut Vintage 1988 Champagne on ice with three flutes. Indeed, she wanted to impress the best. She also had the red carpet out, the parking lot was closed off with signs telling regular clients that they were closed this afternoon for and private event. Shasta phoned Big Mo and Nick earlier after Stacey left to make sure they were suited and booted at the entrance for when Mr. Delowe arrived. Even though he has been to her club on many occasions before, this was the first time he was coming for business. She wanted everything to be perfect. Mr. Delowe was giving Shasta almost $50 million dollars to open Luxury Phase 2 and they had only one more contract to sign before it became official. She didn't want anything to go fucked up. Luxury Phase 2 was then next chapter in her life—only for the super-rich and elite.

Mr. Delowe pulled up in the "Midnight Rider" for those of you who don't know what that is…Google it. Shasta mouth dropped to the floor, never had she seen anything like this before in her life. She thought to herself, all this for little ol' me.

Mr. Delowe chauffer was a biker type muthafucka with the matching jacket. You could tell he was strapped. He walked quickly around to open the door for Mr. Delowe and his entourage. Shasta counted at least thirty niggas with him. In a panic, she hurriedly got on the phone and called Stacey.

Before Stacey could say hello, Shasta was screaming demands through the phone.

"I need you to get 50 girls here now!" demanded Shasta.

"Okay. You okay?"

"No. I'm freaking the fuck out. I thought Mr. Delowe was coming alone. He has a whole fucking entourage and I ain't got not one dancer in this motherfucka."

TWO TIMES BETRAYED

"Okay. Doing it now," replied Stacey.

"And call Melody and that other chick I hired last week as a bartender. I forget her name. Just call her. I need everybody here in like…NOW!"

"Okay, I got you. I texting Maui now. She say she five minutes away."

"And get DJ Kash here. Nick gone hold it down till he gets here."

"Okay."

They both hung up.

Thank God Shasta already had the music blasting, so the vibe was straight when the entourage starting coming in. Shasta sat in her office and nervously watched on her cameras Mr. Delowe's entrance after his entourage, accompanied with two of his private security personnel and the beautiful, Ms. Dahlia; his trophy wife and business advisor.

Mr. Delowe had one of his security personnel stay at the entrance while Big Mo escorted him and Dahlia to Shasta's office. Everything was falling into place. Shasta looked on as she saw Melody and what's her face make they way behind the bar, at the same time Maui and nine other girls were gyrating their way through the crowd of thirsty, horny ass niggas. Relieved and thankful she made the decision to give Stacey more responsibility. She really came through for her this time, especially at the VERY last minute.

Big Mo knocked on Shasta's door.

"It's open."

Big Mo extended the door for Mr. Delowe and Dahlia to enter. He closed the door behind him and stood in front of it.

Shasta greeted the both of them.

"Hello, and how are you?" said Shasta extended her hand to Mr. Delowe.

"Dahlia, this is Shasta Davis the owner of this nice establishment, and Shasta meet Dahlia, my wife and business advisor," introduced Mr. Delowe

Lynise

Even though Shasta had already known who she was, she just wasn't expecting to be meeting her.

"How do you do?" said the ladies as they shook hands.

"Please, have a seat," said Shasta directing them to the cashmere sofa.

"Can I pour you both a glass of champagne?" asked Shasta.

"Of course," replied Dahlia.

Dahlia took a sip of the champagne, then smiled.

"This tastes expensive," said Dahlia.

Shasta picked up the champagne bottle and turned toward Dahlia so she could see who it was by.

"Good choice," said Dahlia.

"Thank you."

Shasta also offered her and Mr. Delowe some of the strawberries and cheeses she had prepared on solid gold saucers adjacent to the serving tray.

Shasta couldn't help but stare at her and Mr. Delowe and Dahlia. She had never seen Dahlia and it had been months since her last meeting with Mr. Delowe. There recent communication had been by email or Skype, and she damn show didn't remember him looking this good the last time she saw him. She had to catch herself from staring. He was indeed a gorgeous, chocolate, tall man. He stood six feet even; slightly muscular, beautiful skin, perfect white teeth and hazel eyes that complimented his beautifully structured face. He was dressed in an all-black Gucci suit personally designed by Tom Ford and matching Gucci dress shoes.

His wife Dahlia wasn't bad on the eyes either. She wasn't as tall as Mr. Delowe, thank God. She stood around 5'6", 5'7" without heels on. From Shasta's time in Miami she could tell Dahlia was of the Caribbean descendant, maybe Brazilian. She had long, beautiful, auburn red dyed hair. Very petite in shape, with just enough ass to satisfy a black man; with an average size bust and green eyes. Not sure if they were real or not, but they complimented the aqua turquoise

TWO TIMES BETRAYED

Dolce & Gabbana baby doll dress she was sporting. Right along with her white and gold Prada bag with matching sandals.

Dahlia and Mr. Delowe for sure looked like the power couple they were. Like and spitting image of Beyoncé' and Jay- Z, only they weren't entertainers, they were investors.

They all chatted a little off subject for a while. They discussed everything from politics to music before they eventually got down to business.

"Are we expecting someone else for this meeting?" asked Dahlia staring at Shasta's surveillance of the parking lot.

Shasta turned around to an all-white Lexus GS 350 parked in the front of the club. They all watched the screen waiting to see who it was to get out the car.

It was Stacey. A huge smile lit up Shasta's face, yet out the corner of her eye she could see Dahlia's face dashed with ah slick frown of jealousy.

"Who is that?" asked Mr. Delowe not taking his eyes off the camera.

"That's my right hand, Stacey Le'Velle," said Shasta proudly.

Not only did Ms. Stacey upgrade her whip, she upgraded herself. She stepped out her brand new Lexus rocking a black and white pin stripe Versace suit. Dark shades. Shasta could also tell she was wearing a pair of Jimmy Choo stilettos only because she had just bought the same pair two days ago. Shasta had never really noticed how beautiful Stacey was until this very moment.

Stacey's caramel complexion did wonders for her new and improved look. She quickly reminded her of Kila's figure, minus the evil and greed that ran through her veins. Stacey hair was pint back in a neat sophisticated bun.

Nick didn't even realize who she was at first.

"I'm sorry man. This is a private event," said Nick, not allowing Stacey to pass by.

"Fool, it's me," Stacey lowered her shades.

Lynise

Nick lowered his too.

"Damn girl, it show is. Fuck. You clean up nice," said Nick lustfully licking his lips.

"You gone let me in or what?" asked Stacey smiling.

"Yeah, yeah. Hell yeah, I'll let all that ass in anywhere," replied Nick watching Stacey walk off.

"I ain't even know she had all that ass back there," said Nick out loud.

Stacey made her way to Shasta's office where Big Mo and one of the men in black was on guard.

Big Mo in attention glanced over at Stacey.

"Stacey?" said Big Mo

"Yeah, it's me."

"Damn."

"Yeah, yeah. I know."

"I clean up nice," said Stacey.

"You damn sho' do," replied Big Mo with a smile.

Stacey entered Shasta's office and was immediately introduced to Mr. Delowe and Dahlia.

Dahlia still had a slick look of jealously on her face she so desperately tried to hide with a smile. Shasta grabbed another flute out of the pantry and poured Stacey a glass of champagne.

"Now we can get down to business," said Shasta with a higher feeling of authority.

"Yes, we can," said Mr. Delowe, obviously still staring at Stacey.

They talked numbers for the next hour and a half and before the meeting was over they all had a clear understanding of what was expected of each other, and what was to take place over the next few months. Mr. Delowe made arrangements to be in the country for the grand opening. He put his John Hancock, along with Shasta's on the last of the contracts. They were officially in business together, with her still being full owner of her first club Luxury.

Mr. Delowe and Dahlia said their good-byes to Shasta and Stacey.

TWO TIMES BETRAYED

They both stood outside and watched as Mr. Delowe, Dahlia, the men in black, and there entourage ride off in the "Midnight Rider."

Moments later, Shasta and Stacey were back in her office, by that time Big Mo, Nick, Melody and Maui were posted up in there on the couch.

"Ooh...ooh look at you, Miss thang," said Shasta as she smacked Stacey on the ass.

Stacey just stood there blushing feeling real good about herself.

"I know, you don't see her," said Big Mo.

"Shit I do, real clear," said Nick.

"Yeah, honey, you look really nice," said Melody.

"Um, huh. She do don't she?" said Maui.

"Thank you, thank you," said Stacey.

Shasta grabbed four more flutes out of the pantry and passed them to each of them.

"So, I bet y'all all wondering why Ms. Stacey all razzled and dazzled."

Nick and Big Mo still staring at Stacey.

"Well, to fill your curiosity. Ms. Stacey Le'Velle has been promoted to my right hand, and will be in charge of the day to day operations of Luxury 1 & 2," said Shasta.

They all started clapping for her in light of the good news.

"That ain't it. I have something for the four of you as well."

Shasta reached in her desk and pulled out four envelopes. She had come to the decision of promoting them instantly when she saw how quickly they came to her aid today. She only wished that Carmen could have been a part of this, but she knew that she wasn't in the right frame of mind to take on any more responsibility. She would be straight anyway.

She gave Nick and Big Mo there envelopes first.

"I'm promoting you two to head of security. Nick, you're going to stay here and Big Mo you're going to Phase 2."

They both opened the envelopes a saw a check for $50,000.

Lynise

"Damn. For real?" asked Nick.

"Good looking," said Big Mo.

"Yeah, y'all both deserve it."

They both hugged her.

"Now for you Melody. I'm making you Manager of all the bartenders for both clubs."

Shasta gave her, her envelope. Inside was a check for $50,000 too.

"Get the fuck outta here!" screamed Melody jumping up and down like she just hit the lottery, hugging Shasta.

"And for you, baby girl. My Maui. I'm making you Stacey's Assistant. I know firsthand how well y'all work together," said Shasta as she gave Maui a check for $75,000.

"Oh my fucking God!"

"I love working here," said Maui, hugging Shasta along with Melody.

"Let's make a toast," said Shasta.

Stacey poured them all champagne and they held their flutes in the air.

"You do the honors, Ms. Stacey "New Money" Le'Velle," said Shasta.

"Of course."

"To making more money than any of us could ever spend!"

"Hell yeah!" They all said in harmony.

They all toasted and hugged. You could see the feeling of good days to come ahead on each of their faces. Shasta stood back and admired Stacey's transformation, she looked at all of them in approval of the decisions she had made today. There was nothing getting in her way, she wasn't going to let anyone keep her from getting to the top.

Except Valerie, aka Monica.

CHAPTER 10

Cybercam1908

"In the club goin hard, niggas know I got them racks. In the kitchen whipping hard, niggas know I got dat sack," Valerie sang along to Yo Gotti in her car on the way home from a long, prosperous night at the club.

Valerie had done stacked up at least 40k since she had been employed with Shasta. She had upgraded her wardrobe and whip as well. Not as exclusive as Stacey, but she was riding clean. A 2013 candy apple red Chevy Camaro, Big's favorite car. She also had a cute little condo, which was a major step up from Lindsey Street and about twenty minutes away from Luxury. Although she was living better than she did in Atlanta, she still felt sour about the fact that her living arrangements were nowhere near the lifestyle she had grew accustomed to with Big. That reason alone drove hate through her veins for Shasta. Valerie, aka Monica, felt Shasta stole her life from right up under her.

"Blind rage will have a person thinking they entitled to shit that really never belonged to them."

Hoodknomics

Valerie pulled up in her garage, where she entered through the kitchen and was greeted by her pitch black Yorky puppy she called

Lynise

Big Jr.

"Hi baby, Mommy's home," said Valerie to her new puppy roommate. She watched as he ran back and forth between her legs.

"Are you hungry?"

Valerie bent down to pick up Big Jr. She prepared his gourmet dish by Three Dog Bakery and watched him eat for a while before she headed to the sofa and indulged in her daily happiness of cocaine. Ironically, most people do lines and get amped the fuck up; she did them and could go to sleep. Guess you could say she was a recreational user; eight times a week. Weirdly enough, she could also eat full meals on the dope. That is a prime example that drugs affect everyone in a different way. After a few lines, she opened up her laptop and checked her emails only to see she had two from cybercam1908.

The first read:

Hey doll, Just checking up on you. Haven't heard from you in a while. Hope CT's treating you well. Here if you need me.

-Cybercam1908

"Aww, that's so sweet," said Valerie.

She opened the next one, and it read:

Bored without another thing to do, I've been sitting here thinking of our last encounter. Pondering on why you paid me almost $2,000 dollars for information you could have clearly accessed yourself. Then it dawn on me, all public records keep a log of all search inquires. You had me search for her because you didn't want a trail that you were looking for her. Looking for the young lady, 'Ms. Shasta Davis' that you had me track for you and who you didn't want anyone else to know you were searching for, made me curious about her and led me to further investigation.

Ms. Valerie Alexis Carter (courtesy of me) or should I say Mrs. Monica Charmaine Reed, widow of Anthony "Big" Reed.

Valerie eyes got bigger and her mouth dropped wider as she continued to read.

It read further:

TWO TIMES BETRAYED

See, I've been digging, guess we can blame it on the curious mind. Two years ago you were married to Anthony "Big" Reed, who Shasta gunned down in a Miami garage after her and her associate Kila robbed him and his friends for over $500 thousand dollars. The investigation went nowhere. Ultimately, she got off and used the 500k to start up the fine establishment you currently work at today. We can both see where this is going. You're looking for revenge. I can help.

Cybercam1908

Valerie's heart was beating fast as fuck; she poured out her entire box of happiness and filled her living room table with lines. She also threw back a Molly.

"Fuck! Fuck! I hope this bitch don't think he finna black mail me!" yelled Valerie. Pacing her floor thowed, because if he did, the only thing she could do was leave town. Cybercam1908 really had her in a fucked-up predicament.

Cybercam1908 knew everything about her, and she didn't know shit about him. Hell, she didn't even know if it was a male or a female on the other end of the screen. Valerie figured she had no other choice but to respond. She took a deep breath and instant messaged cybercam1908 this time.

Monica1987: You there?
Cybercam1908: Sure am my dear.
Cybercam1908: You get my emails?
Monica1987: I did.
Monica1987: What do you want?
Cybercam1908: Nothing dear. I'm offended. I only wanted to extend my much needed services to you ☺.

Valerie thought to herself, *I don't need this muthafucka no mo'*.

Monica1987: I got it under control, but thanks for your concern.
Cybercam1908: That could be true, but my homework tells me that you want Ms. Shasta to feel the exact same ending your Big faced. Just to be honest, that ain't gone work. Guns are messy. There's plenty ways to skin a cat.

Lynise

Deep into thought, Valerie felt that cybercam muthafucka was hijacking her thoughts. As much as she wanted to blow Shasta brains out in a parking lot the same way she did Big. She knew the chances of that happening were slim to none.

Cybercam1908: *U there? U there?*

Monica1987: *Yes. How do you recommend I solve my problem then?*

Cybercam1908: *I got something smooth and simple in mind, however it's gone cost you.*

Monica1987: *How much?*

Cybercam1908: *15k*

Monica1987: *Done.*

Cybercam1908: *Do you still have my wire information?*

Monica1987: *Yes.*

Cybercam1908: *Transfer my cash and I'll overnight your solution.*

Monica1987: *You will have it in a few.*

Valerie sits and stares at her laptop hoping Cybercam ain't tryna set her up on some fuck shit.

"What the fuck do I have to lose? I can either see where this shit goes or pack up and leave," said Valerie as she wired Cybercam1908 the money.

"I've come too fucking far to bitch up now. Fuck, It is what it is."

Ding. IM notifies Valerie.

Cybercam1908: *I got it. Thanks. Your solution should arrive in the mail tomorrow, be sure to follow the directions.*

Monica1987: *I'll let you know once I receive it. After that, we're done.*

Cybercam1908: *Aww too bad. I thought we were just entering a new phase in our relationship.*

"Whatever!" said Valerie talking to her laptop.

Monica1987: *Goodbye.*

Valerie ended there chat before she was able to review Cybercam1908's response. She was done playing his game. In fact,

TWO TIMES BETRAYED

once she received her package in the morning, she was packing her shit and moving. Clearing all ties to that muthafucka. In the meantime, she finished the last of her happiness and wiped her table clean—keeping Big Jr. from becoming an addict.

Completely drained from today's events, Valerie picked up her puppy and curled up on her couch, falling asleep listening to Yo Gotti's "I got dat sack" on repeat.

G STREET CHRONICLES
A LITERARY POWERHOUSE
WWW.GSTREETCHRONICLES.COM

Chapter 11

The Grand Opening

Shasta was excited about Luxury Phase 2's grand opening. She had several big wigs flying in from all over the country. She was even more excited, because her most favorite rapper of all time, Young Jeezy, was to be in attendance tonight, as well as some of her other favorites who were going to be performing tonight.

Shasta couldn't wait to see Meek Mills, Freeway, Drake, King Lo, Yo Gotti, Devin Cruise, Luxury Dutch, Wale, Chris Brown and Trey Songz hit the stage. Indeed, it was destined to be a star-studded event, and she had some of the most beautiful girls in the world to accommodate them accordingly.

Shasta's VIP guest list included everyone from Jay-Z, Diddy, Rihana, Paris Hilton, Joseline Hernandez, Stevie J, German Prince Albert courtesy of Mr. Delowe, Ciara, Future, Haitian Fresh, Boosie Bad Ass, Baby, Lil' Wayne, Usher, and of course half the NBA & NFL. Her guest list was stupid. Thankfully, the club was large enough to carter to her entire VIP squad and their egos.

Luxury Phase 2 was three stories high, and over 20,000 square feet of pure bliss. The main floor had six Italian marbled bars designed by Adelina; four stages, two complete changing rooms and twelve closed-off private rooms for VIP Gold Members. It also had

Lynise

an aquatic fish tank that she had built in the walls starting from the first floor to the third, and it had of some of the most amazing tropical fish man had ever seen. The fish were literally hand caught from the waters of Cayo Coco and Bora Bora. The décor for all three floors was a mixture of black and gold it would put you in the mind of the Aurum Lounge back in Atlanta. On the second floor was Shasta's and Stacey's offices; they were detached from where the clientele mingled. This area was exclusively for VIP Platinum members and VIP guests of stature that was more private. It had only three stages, two bars and five of the nationally known, "Fun Rooms." The floor was made of interrogation glass; you could look down but not up. The third floor, which was the roof, was Shasta's favorite, she called it the Wet & Wild section. It was equipped with a pool the shape of a dollar sign, with a floating bar in the middle, surrounded by three Jacuzzi hot tubs. There were five waterfall shower rooms with swings and one cement stage in the middle of the pool. Luxury Phase 2 was, in fact, going to be the hottest Gentlemen's Club on the East coast.

Shasta got to the club several hours early to do a last walk through, just to make sure everything was on point for tonight.

"I can't afford for nothing to go wrong tonight. I got too much riding on this shit, it gotta go smooth," Shasta said, thinking she was alone.

"It won't. Imma make sure of that," Stacey said, sneaking up behind her.

Shasta jumped.

"Damn it girl! You scared the shit outta me," said Shasta as she reached over to embrace Stacey.

"I'm so excited!"

"Me too, honey. I'm excited and nervous. I think I need a drink." Shasta made her way to the bar.

"What time is Melody and Carmen getting here? I told everyone last night I needed them here early."

"Melody is on her way now and Carmen should be here within

the hour." Stacey replied.

"Okay. Cool."

Shasta poured both of them a glass of champagne.

"What about the new hires?" asked Shasta.

"They all should be arriving in the next thirty minutes. I told them if they ain't here by 7:00 p.m. they don't need come."

"Ok. Ok, cool," said Shasta.

"So far so good. Don't worry love, tonight is going to be perfect," said Stacey with confidence.

"It better, way too much money on the line for shit to get fucked up. For real, for real." replied Shasta. "Too many very important people are sliding through; therefore there can't be no FUCK UPS!" said Shasta rambling on.

About thirty minutes later, the staff and patrons began to arrive. Shasta had a line outside the club something serious. She was still extremely nervous as fuck, although her first club did numbers, Phase 2 was a whole new venture with way more money to account for—point blank, period. It had to go right.

"Fuck!" Said Shasta

"Do you see all those people?" said Stacey as her and Shasta viewed the parking lot cameras.

"Girl, is that the news out there?" asked Stacey.

"Hell, yeah! Now that's what I'm talking 'bout!" said Shasta.

"Doors open in twenty minutes. You ready suga?"

"As ready as I'll ever be."

"Well, let's do it then. Your featured girls, Mauy and Valerie, will alternate between floors. I got fifty girls covering the first floor, and the other fifty spread out between the second and third floors," Stacey stated as she watched Shasta still staring at the cameras.

There were so many stretch limousines outside; on top of the news stations, there were magazine paparazzi lined up as well, taking pictures of wheels because no one had gotten out of their vehicles yet.

It was already awesome.

Lynise

Shasta grabbed her earpiece and gave Big Mo and Nick the okay to start letting people in the club. The music was blasting, with Bose surround sound beating through every floor. As the first guest started to enter, Shasta and Stacey eagerly watched the impressions on their faces. She could tell they were pleased as they took their seats and watched the girls slide up and down the polls effortlessly.

Shasta felt like a big ass kid again; and to make matters better, she almost dropped her champagne when she saw her Young Jeezy walk the red carpet down her VIP side.

Stacey studied Shasta's face watching her smile get bigger and bigger.

"Let me guess. The Snowman here, ain't he?"

"I can't believe he actually came through!"

"Oh My God, Oh My God!" Shasta said with excitement.

"Girl, you acting like a real five year old on Christmas day," Stacey laughed.

"You're Shasta Davis. I knew Jeezy was gone come out and support you; plus, he told me he was coming two days ago," said Stacey proudly.

"Really! Get the fuck outa here. I gotta calm down. I'm acting like a real groupie right now." You know you coulda told me!" said Shasta, damn near to tears of happiness.

"I know, but I wanted to surprise you."

Shasta just hugged Stacey.

"Best surprise ever," said Shasta still hugging Stacey.

"Well, you're welcome."

Stacey poured them both another glass of champagne as they continued to watch the rest of the guest enter the club. Everything was in place, and from the looks on everyone's faces they seem to be enjoying themselves thus far.

"It's time to make our rounds now, " said Shasta.

"It sure is," Stacey replied.

"Go get Valerie and Mauy. I want them exclusively for the

TWO TIMES BETRAYED

Snowman's entertainment and whatever else he wants."

"I know he will be pleased with them."

"Okay," said Stacey as she left outa Shasta's office.

A few minutes later, Valerie and Maui were following behind Stacey over to Young Jeezy's VIP booth. Like many of the other VIP's, Jeezy had his own security with him. Shasta walked over to him and sat beside him. Mauy and Valerie kept standing.

"Thank you so much for coming!" yelled Shasta because the music was loud as fuck.

"No problem."

"You gotta straight lil spot here, I'm glad to come support you." Jeezy said, already high as hell.

"Ahh. Thanks brah," said Shasta as she reached over and gave him a hug. She signaled for Maui and Valerie to come closer.

"They are for you," Shasta said.

Jeezy lowered his Ray-Ban's to get a better look, he already had five other dancers in the booth with him. Shasta had Maui and Valerie turn around so he could see how fat they asses were. He approved.

"If you need anything, let them know and they will make it happen."

"Aiight, bet."

Shasta got up to speak with Maui and Valerie.

"Y'all have fun, and I don't think I have to tell y'all to treat right?" said Shasta.

They both shook their heads in agreement.

Shasta disappeared, headed to more booths to personally thank her guest for coming, she rapped with Jay-Z and Yo Gotti for a sec and watched the rest perform. The night went even better than planned. Shasta was told by everyone she encountered that they loved the club, the girls were boasting 'bout how they had never made that much money in one week, let alone one night. Everybody, as far as she could see it, left Luxury Phase 2 happy and fucked up.

The club had made damn near 1.5 million dollars. Shasta's only

Lynise

disappointment was that Mr. Delowe couldn't make it for the grand opening. He was so-called stuck in Paris on another business venture; however, Shasta felt Dahlia had a hand in his absence. Either way it went, she ain't give a fuck, because truth be told, if she kept having profitable nights like this one, she would be closer to paying Mr. Delowe his ten million back, plus major interest a whole lot sooner than later.

Shasta good deal with Dahlia, once that money was paid back she would be sole owner until then, her and Mr. Delowe were in a 50/50 partnership which seemingly came alone with Dahlia.

Chapter 12

After The Grand Opening

"Didn't I tell you the grand opening was gone be turnt up to da muthafuckin max!" said Stacey.

"Hell yeah, love," Shasta replied.

Of course, since things went so well for Luxury Phase 2 first night of business, Shasta wanted to do something nice for her ladies. She treated them all to a day of pampering and relaxation.

"Muthafuckas still tweeting 'bout da grand opening and shit, a week later," said Mauy, checking through her twitter account.

"And I didn't know I could suck that much dick in one night either," laughed Valerie.

Mauy laughed, "Snowman and his whole crew got dick for days."

"Ewwww, y'all nasty," said Shasta and Stacey at the same time.

"I'm proud to be nasty," laughed Mauy.

"Me, too. I came home with almost fifteen fuckin racks just from tips. Outside of the dancing, I'll happily suck da whole crew up. They respect the hustle and I respect them," said Valerie.

They all just busted out laughing while the Asians soaked their hands, feet and placed cucumbers over their eyes.

"Shit, I hear Melody and Carmen went home with a nice check too," said Shasta.

"Speaking of Carmen, has anyone talked to her lately?" asked

Lynise

Stacey.

"Naw," said Valerie and Mauy.

"I called her a few days ago, but she ain't answer. Knowing her and what she got going on with Nico, he probably done beat her ass again and she too embarrassed to tell someone," stated Shasta.

"Damn. He be jumping on her like dat? Dats why she don't like no damn body," said Maui.

"Naw boo, she like everyone else. Except for yo' ass!" Melody said, cutting her eyes at Maui in loving irritation.

The ladies looked up and saw Melody; after they embraced, one of the attendants set her up and poured her a glass of champagne.

"Hey suga pie, 'bout time you showed yo ass up," said Shasta.

"Hey love," replied Melody.

Maui being the kid she is, jumps out the hot tub and hugs Melody.

"Alright, alright, hey to you too. Let me go child."

"Stacey got the hot tub to get Melody's glass of champagne from the bar the attendants left for her, while tapping up the other ladies' drinks.

"What I miss?" asked Melody.

"Shit nothing, we was just talking 'bout how many dicks Valerie and Mauy can suck and how no one can reach Carmen ass," said Shasta.

"Damn, just put it out there like that then," laughed Valerie.

"Well, I hope you ladies gargled afterwards." said Melody.

Stacey almost choked, she was laughing so hard.

"See, this the shit here I love. We all getting along, getting money, fine ass fuck with no bull shit on top," said Shasta.

"I'll toast to dat," said Mauy.

"Yo' ass will toast to any damn thing," Stacey replied.

The ladies held their glasses up.

"To more money, fuck a problem, I got that check to solve it!" said Shasta.

"Me, too," said Stacey.

TWO TIMES BETRAYED

"And so do I!" said Melody.

"Shit, me too." Valerie added.

"Well, I ain't broke either!" said Mauy laughing.

"Something is seriously wrong with you." Stacey smiled, looking at Shasta.

"You just now knowing that?" asked Shasta.

"Yeah, hell yeah."

Kicking it, laughing and chopping it up, they couldn't help but notice that Carmen still hadn't showed up yet.

"Melody? For real, for real. When was the last time you heard from Carmen?" asked Shasta.

"I haven't heard from her since the grand opening."

"I've called her a few times, but she ain't return my calls yet. Hell, I just figured, as usual Nico got her cut off from the world."

Looking puzzled, Shasta nodded and then took another sip of her champagne.

"Yeah, but it ain't like her not to return my calls. For real, for real, she ah at least text me ah something," said Shasta.

"I know," said Melody.

They all had a sudden look of worry on their faces. Shasta got out of the hot tub and the rest of the ladies followed suit.

"We goin' over there," stated Shasta.

"You took the thought right out of my head," said Stacey.

A few minutes later, they were all dressed and loaded in Shasta's Range Rover headed to Carmen's house. When they got there, they were greeted by the Police, Fire Department, EMT, and Coroner's Dept.

They all stared at each other in fear thinking the worst; as Shasta drove closer they could see the yellow tape blocking off Carmen's building. Shasta saw Ms. Caroline with her head buried in her son Mark's arms, crying hysterically. Shasta's heart dropped to her stomach; before the car was parked, she, Stacey and Melody jumped out the car and ran over to Ms. Caroline. Mark gave Shasta a look

Lynise

in her eyes, and from that moment she already knew what was up. Melody saw the tears form in Shasta's eyes, and immediately she broke down.

"No, no, no!" cried Melody falling to the ground. Mauy ran up and just held her as tight as she could—given their relationship.

Ms. Caroline looked up and saw Shasta was there.

"He killed her! He finally beat her to death!" cried Ms. Caroline.

Shasta just stood there with tears running down her face as she watched the Medical Examiners roll Carmen's body out of her apartment into the Coroner's van.

Carmen's Uncle Mel, who had only been in town since the night before had arrived. His intentions were to surprise his niece of his permanent relocation to Connecticut. Uncle Mel was the last of her mother's side that wasn't dead or in jail. Uncle Mel couldn't contain himself as he watched the Medical Examiner put his niece into the van. It took six policemen to keep him from attacking the carriers.

"What the fuck! What the fuck!"

"Who did this to her?" cried her Uncle.

If you've never heard screams from a grown man in pure distraught, I wouldn't be able to describe the pain he's feeling right now.

Uncle Mel fell to the ground, crying. Ms. Caroline and Mark went to do their best to console him, but there wasn't anything they could do to mend the pain, so they just held him as tight as they could. Valerie walked over to Shasta and held her hand. Emotionless, Valerie stood there with Shasta as they all watched the coroner pull off with Carmen's body. Shasta yanked her hand away from Valerie and charged Mark with her fist balled up in fighting position.

"You said you was gone handle it!"

"You said wasn't nothing else gone happen to her!" cried Shasta beating Mark in the chest.

Mark grabbed her wrist and looked her straight in the eyes feeling bad about being too late.

"I'm sorry Shasta. I'm so, so sorry Shasta," cried Mark remorsefully.

Shasta watched as the tears fell down Mark's face uncontrollably. She stopped hitting him and allowed for him to embrace her. Weakened by sadness, they both fell to ground holding each other and crying in agony.

Valerie stood alone looking at everyone else around her. Everyone else was crying and full of emotions, except her. She barely even broke a tear. With everything going on around her the only thing she could focus on was the fact that Shasta was finally mourning a loss just as she had. Valerie loved every bit of it, it took every bone in her face to keep her from smiling, at the end of the day she couldn't hide the smirk.

In the midst of everything, while Mauy was consoling Melody. Mauy saw the obvious smirk of pleasure on Valerie's face. The two of them locked eyes, and Valerie gave Mauy the most evil look—as if she could be next type look. Mauy looked away pretending she didn't see anything.

The Detectives attempted to question Ms. Caroline and Uncle Mel, but didn't get far. They were just too heartbroken to answer any questions at this point. Mark picked Shasta up off the ground and helped her to the passenger side of her truck.

"Imma kill that pussy nigga, Shasta. I promise you on everything I love most. That fuck nigga gone get his. I promise!" said Mark, wiping the last of tears from his face.

Shasta leaned her head against her seats head rest and just stared out the window completely heartbroken. Melody hugged and kissed Ms. Caroline as she and Uncle Mel left to go inside the house before she made her way back to the truck with Mark and Shasta. Stacey never got out the truck during the whole ordeal. She was used to watching the ones closet to her die, she grew up in Oakland, California, so this was nothing new to her. The only reason she shed a tear, was because the pain she saw on Shasta's face as they rolled Carmen's body out. Stacey sat in the back of the truck and turned up

Lynise

the bottle of champagne feeling numb to it all.

Valerie and Mauy was the last to get in the truck. Valerie tormented Mauy with an evil look in her eyes, only because Mauy saw the real her by accident. When they entered the truck, Mauy made sure Melody was sitting between the two of them. Mark was still standing by Shasta's side, wiping her face.

"Are you sure you good to drive?" asked Mark.

"Yeah," Stacey was broken.

"How 'bout I drive?" said Mauy, looking at Valerie and desperately wanting to get from in the back seat with Valarie.

"Naw, I'm good," said Stacey.

"To be on the safe side…just let Mauy drive."

"Okay."

Stacey switched seats with Mauy.

Mark reached in and kissed Shasta on the forehead.

"Take her home, y'all chill with her tonight. I'll be over soon as I make sure my Momma and Uncle Mel straight," said Mark.

"Okay," answered Mauy.

Mark watched as Mauy pulled off with Shasta and the crew.

"I shoulda been dead that nigga ass!" yelled Mark hitting the top of his car.

The police tried to clear the crowd, but there wasn't an easy thing to do. There were so many of Carmen's friends and neighbors still on the block it was hard for the news team to get through the scene. Out of all the people out there outraged about tonight's events, Nico was nowhere to be found. Carmen had been dead for two days before her body was discovered and Nico's phone was disconnected. No one knew where he was and his family damn sho' wasn't answering any questions. Lost for now is what he was, but that was only temporary.

Chapter 13

The End Is Near

Preacher, preaching and choir singing.
    Valerie came home from Carmen's funeral to an FedEx package on her door step; she picks it up and carries it in the house hoping that it's finally her solution from Cybercam1908.

She ain't wanna get her hopes up high, at the same time she wasn't expecting anything else in delivery. This wasn't the first time Cybercam1908 was late with information, at the same time she couldn't help but feel he had conned her. Shit, it had been three weeks since she shot him a check for an overnight delivery.

Valerie entered her condo and placed the box on her dining room table. Throwing her handbag on the floor, anxious to get off the unwanted funeral clothes, she began daydreaming, in satisfaction, of the distraught face of Shasta. She poured herself a glass of wine before she decided to open her up mail. Getting fully comfortable, Valerie kicked off her whore shoes which she felt were funeral appropriate, and grabbed her package.

"This bitch...mystery bitch, betta be official," said Valerie as she picked up Big's picture and routinely kissed it.

Valerie opened up the package and saw five vials of an unfamiliar liquid substance, along with and letter from Cybercam1908.

It read:

Lynise

Greetings Love,

We see who getting money now. You haven't been bugging me like before, but that's cool. I apologize for the delay in product. I had some difficult strings to pull, no worries though. You have the best in your presence now. I also sent you some extra just in case you fucked up in the administering process. My treat. All you have to do is mix this substance with one of her favorite drinks and you all set. You can, from that point, sit back and quickly watch her painfully die to your satisfaction. There's no need for you to know what it is, just sit back and watch it work.

Yours truly,
Cybercam1908

Valerie immediately opened the package after she read the contents of the letter.

"This shit betta work." Valerie examines the vials.

Placing each one of them on the table, going into deep thought. She was anxious to use one of them. Even if it was just a tester.

"In due time bitch. In due time!" said Valerie staring at one of many of Big's pictures around the house.

You would think that with how close she had grown with the ladies and the check she was bringing to the club over the last six months, the women at the club would have known where she lived, yet none of them had ever been to her house. Valerie, aka Monica, had so many pictures of Big all around her house it looked like a hit and run shrine you would see on the highway. She had more pictures of Big than she had of her own damn self. Fucking crazy.

Valerie fed Big Jr. while she happily smiled herself to her bedroom. She locked away the vials in her closet safe then finished undressing and jumped onto her Ralph Lauren bed set. Falling asleep with pure hate happiness in mind, she was ever so more confident that her plans were quickly flowing into place. She had Shasta in the state of mind she needed and wanted her in before she was ready to attack.

TWO TIMES BETRAYED

Valerie was slowly accomplishing her demented ass goals, along with the help of out the blue situations of her peers that she took advantage of. Indeed, she was happy Shasta was suffering, and in her eyes, this was just the beginning. It was really time to go to work. It was really time for her to wrap this shit up.

G STREET CHRONICLES
A LITERARY POWERHOUSE
WWW.GSTREETCHRONICLES.COM

Chapter 14

Done Mourning

Still fucked up about Carmen's death, Shasta was finally in the right frame of mind to re-open Luxury Phase 1 & 2, along with making sure Nico was seen about. Shasta managed to get herself out of bed, and made her way to her kitchen to attempt to re-commit herself to her daily morning ritual of Mojo juice. She couldn't. Instead, she poured herself a straight shot of Ciroc. She hadn't felt this close to anyone since her friendship with Kila, which was understandable considering how so horribly that ended . She was close to no one. I guess being a victim of abuse and past memories of Big Chris, she felt ah special kinda bond with Carmen.

Shasta put her battery back in her phone and plugged it into the charger she kept in the kitchen. She had completely cut herself off from the world the past couple weeks. She needed a break from all the media attention Carmen's death was getting, only because it was leaked that she was an employee of Luxury, and of course they assumed it was a disgruntle patron that killed her. Either way, she wasn't up for questions and speculations about bullshit.

Scrolling down her call log, she saw several missed calls and voicemails from Mark and Stacey. She dialed Mark's number and he picked up on the first ring.

"Are you okay?" Mark asked before saying hello.

Lynise

"Yeah, I'm fine," said Shasta, not wanting to discuss herself at all.
"I need you to come over."
"I'm on my way, be there in twenty minutes."
"K."

Mark pulled up exactly twenty minutes later. He had an Auto Detail shop around the corner from her neighborhood. He faithfully went to work at his shops every day since Carmen's death, hoping Shasta would call. Knowing that with all the other shops he had spread across Connecticut, he never had to spend too much time at just one. There was nothing he wouldn't do for her, matter of fact he loved her first. He loved her before Big Chris got her.

Shasta was already on the porch when Mark pulled up in his Ferrari. Mark got the car and walked straight towards her. She didn't look herself at least not the Shasta he was used to seeing. She sat on the porch in a long house rob, bare feet, hair pushed up in a bonnet, with a full glass of Ciroc in one hand, and Loud in the next.

Carmen's death really hit Shasta hard, only because she had promised that Nico would never put his hands on her again. This was a promise she felt that should not have been broken, this was a problem she felt that for sure could have been solved. Now at the end of the day, Carmen and the unborn child they were made aware of are both dead. That shit hurt her.

Mark walked up and sat beside her on the porch, not saying anything, just watching the kids ride their bikes and play carelessly. Shasta had made arrangements for Lil' Chris to go down South for the summer with Auntie Nancy. She knew shit was about to get crazy, and she didn't want her son apart of it. It was bad enough she had the news outside her house every day and night.

Mark reached over and grabbed the bottle of Ciroc and hit it cowboy style.

"How you holding up, baby girl?" asked Mark.

"Shit, you can't tell. Look at me." Shasta pulled off a faint laugh.

Mark reached over and grabbed her hand.

TWO TIMES BETRAYED

"I know I let you down, but for real, let me know if you need anything. I got you," said Mark.

"Ha. I need Nico kicking dirt just like Carmen. Can you arrange that!"

"It's done."

"It shoulda been done!" yelled Shasta as she snatched her hand away from Mark's hand.

"I know, I know," said Mark with a regretful sadness in his voice. "I know."

Tears began to roll down Shasta's face again. From the puffiness of her eyes she had been crying prior to Mark's arrival.

"We should have done something."

"She was pregnant," said Shasta, burying her face in her hands.

"Shasta. I'm sorry. God knows I am," said Mark.

Shasta wiped the tears from her eyes and jumped up out of her chair as if nothing was wrong. The hard mentality in her tried its best to shake off the loss.

"I'm good. I'm good," said Shasta going into the house.

Mark just looked at her knowing she wasn't good. He knew that it was just a front, he remembered the ass whoopings she used to take from Big Chris from back in the day. Mark sat for a minute before he followed behind Shasta to the living room. He watched her as she grabbed a box off the table full of Loud. Shasta rolled her blunt, hoping to calm herself down.

"You know, Nico ain't even a suspect in her death?"

"Naw, I ain't hear dat."

"Yeah, word is he was at his shop fucking off with some other hoe while Carmen was being beat to death."

"At least that's what the news is saying."

"Don't stress 'bout that shit. Imma get him."

"Yeah," said Shasta sarcastically.

Mark grabbed Shasta's face so she was looking him directly in his eyes.

Lynise

"Imma get him."

Shasta jerked away.

"Okay."

Shasta passed Mark the blunt. Choking off the smoke.

"Did you hear the bullshit about Nico paying for the funeral?" said Mark passing Shasta back the blunt.

"I heard."

"I ain't see the muthafucka there, but word on the street, he was at Uncle Mel's house afterwards"

"I heard that too," said Mark.

"It's crazy how a muthafucka be so distraught at first, but later kicking it with the Devil."

"That junkie ass nigga came all the way up here from the "A" for hand out," said Mark.

"I know. I remember Carmen saying something about him before he got outta prison."

"It's cool though, he can get it too!" said Shasta passing the blunt back to Mark.

"Right."

"It's crazy, cuz; I been hearing a lot of shit lately."

"Like?"

"Nico done put Uncle Mel up in an expensive ass flat on the Eastside."

"How, when 12 came to interview him the next day, he kicked it like they never used to fight at all, and I'm like why the fuck are they even questioning him. His ass just got out of prison. He ain't even been up here a fucking week."

"Bullshit! Are you fucking kidding me?" stated Shasta.

"I wish I was," said Mark. "That's just what they saying out there."

"So, you mean to tell me this nigga would rather take a check from the nigga who killed his niece than bury him?" asked Shasta.

"Seems that way." Mark passed the blunt back to Shasta.

"If it was up to me, his ass could get that business too. For real,

TWO TIMES BETRAYED

for real."

"One duck at a time," replied Mark.

"Yeah, whatever. Long as the first dead duck is Nico." said Shasta, hitting the last of the Kush. They both laid back on the couch high as fuck. Mark could tell Shasta was feeling a lot better than she was when he had first arrived. Shasta reached over and grabbed Mark's hand and held it. They both just sat there high and in silence listening to Pandora play through her Boze surround sound in the back ground. They didn't realize how quickly content they had become in each other's company until Ariel walked through the front door. Shasta still didn't notice Ariel in her house until she heard the door slam shut. Mark jumped up with his hand on his pistol, staring at the white girl wondering who she was and why the fuck she just walked in like that.

Shasta saw that Mark was on edge, she pushed him back into the couch. Gesturing that he relax and cool the look of suspicion he wore across his face.

"Hey love," greeted Shasta to Ariel. "I thought you were out of town."

"I was doll, noisy Ms. Lena called me and told me about all the chaos going on at your club. I didn't believe her at first, but when I couldn't get through to you I took the first flight back from Mumbai. I've been trying to get back to check on you for the last few days," said Ariel.

"How are you? Are you okay? Can I do anything?" asked Ariel, squeezing between Mark and Shasta.

"Slow down girl. I'm fine and it wasn't at neither of my clubs. It was domestic," replied Shasta.

"Domestic?" said Ariel puzzled.

"A good friend of mine was beat to death."

"No..." said Ariel sympathetically.

Shasta and Ariel's relationship was strictly kiddie world, she didn't discuss her club life with her and Ariel didn't discuss her escort business with Shasta.

Lynise

Mark still sitting, watched Ariel closely.

"Should I call someone? Is that cock sucker dead? Just tell me what can I do," said Ariel rambling on again.

By that last statement Ariel made, Mark's tension relaxed.

"Naw, doll it's being taken care of," replied Shasta.

"Okay."

"You know I'm here for you if you need me."

"Yes. I do." Shasta and Ariel embraced each other.

Ariel got up off the couch and focused her attention to Mark once again. He was still focused on who the fuck she was as well. Shasta could tell from looking at both of their faces that they were in *who the fuck is this* zone.

"My bad."

"Mark, this is my neighbor Ariel. She keeps Lil' Chris from time to time."

"Ariel, this is Mark."

They shook hands.

"Nice to meet you," replied Ariel.

"Same here," said Mark.

Ariel focused her attention back to Shasta. Clearly feeling the awkwardness, Shasta jumped gear.

"Thank you so much for checking in on me."

"Lady bug, you should've known I was coming." Ariel grabbed Shasta's hand.

"Imma walk you out," said Shasta, leaving Mark on the couch.

"Okay." Ariel walked toward the door to leave without saying goodbye.

Shasta walked Ariel all the way to gates or her driveway. Knowing that Ariel had more questions to ask, and she didn't want Mark feeling no extra kinda way about them.

"Who is he?" asked Ariel as if she couldn't wait to get that question out.

"Just ah childhood friend," replied Shasta.

TWO TIMES BETRAYED

"Well, he looks like trouble, and affection."

"Don't you go mixing business with pleasure, we all know where that leads to. Trust me I know, doll."

"Really, it ain't like that. He's a friend."

"Okay," said Ariel skeptically

"For real love, he's just here to solve a problem, he should have solved weeks ago."

Ariel reached in and gave Shasta a long hug.

"You're staying over my house tonight. The boys are gone and I'm not taking no for an answer. Be over here soon as your friend leaves," demanded Ariel.

Shasta couldn't help but to agree.

"Okay."

Ariel hugged her one last time then exited her driveway over to her home. Shasta turned around to see Mark walking out her house in the direction to his car.

"You gone?" asked Shasta.

"Yeah. I'm sorry all this shit happened, for real shawty. Nico will be in a body bag next time you hear from me," said Mark as he got into his Ferrari and pulled off without saying bye.

Shasta didn't want him to feel like Carmen's death was his fault, although she was mad that Nico hadn't been sent about, all she could do was just wave her hand saying goodbye. Alone again, Shasta sat on the porch and watched as Mark's car got smaller and smaller as he drove off further and further, and his music got softer and softer. She didn't blame him, she blamed herself.

G STREET CHRONICLES
A LITERARY POWERHOUSE
WWW.GSTREETCHRONICLES.COM

Chapter 15

It's Get'n Hot In The Kitchen

"I got all them hoes throw'd in the blender. This bitch so fucked up in the head 'bout Carmen, she actually closed down both clubs!" laughed Monica. Damn, and that ain't even the best part. They all think Nico killed her. What can I say? When you're good, you're good," Monica said out loud, talking to Big Jr.

"It was so easy. The stupid bitch ain't even see it coming."

Monica sat up in her bed allowing Big Jr. to lick her face. She grabbed the picture of Big she kept on the night stand, and began talking to it.

"Big, you woulda been so proud of me. I got the Detectives thinking it was a robbery gone bad. I wouldn't be surprised if her boyfriend, Nico, turnt up dead somewhere after this shit."

Carmen's death was still all over the news. Monica turned her T.V. up to get the latest. They was still talking about the same shit, only addition was now Detectives were releasing to the public that they found and unexplained fingerprint. They would not say where about in the apartment they found it at though. They also reported that the District Attorney is in the process of having Shasta, her entire staff and membership list served with subpoenas in order to start ruling people out as suspects. Starting with the local clientele.

"Fuck!" said Monica out loud, scaring Big Jr.

Lynise

"This shit cannot be happening!"

Monica quickly got up out of bed, got dressed and headed straight for the club. If all was about to go to shit, she could at least grab her file, and get outta of town before it was her turn to get fingerprinted.

When Monica pulled up she saw Shasta's Range Rover parked out front. Monica hit the steering wheel in anger and panic.

"Damn it! I thought this bitch wasn't coming back until Friday," said Monica talking to herself.

A nervous wreck, she needed to calm down. Monica hit the sack of cocaine she had stashed under her seat. She took two heavy bumps before she went in the club. She was immediately greeted by Stacey.

"Hey, girl," said Stacey.

"Hey," replied Valerie

"What you doing here? I thought you weren't coming in tonight," asked Stacey.

"I wasn't, but I got tired of sitting up in the house," answered Valerie.

"Well, Shasta's back."

"I thought so, I saw her truck parked out front," said Valerie, looking a little shaky.

Stacey noticed.

"Are you sure you good to work tonight?" asked Stacey.

"Yeah, I'm straight."

"Cause you know we got it covered. Plus, girl you can use the time off. Yo' ass always working," said Stacey.

"Naw, I'm good. I like working."

"Are they really finna fingerprint all of us?" asked Valerie trying to change the subject.

"It seems that way. Some Detectives were in here earlier taking boxes of employee records," said Stacey.

"Have they got all of them?" asked Valerie.

"Naw. They just got the list off employees who started at Phase 2, they will be back for Phase 1 sooner than later."

TWO TIMES BETRAYED

"We haven't been issued a subpoena yet for the membership list, but the way they been in and out of here that ah be next. For sure."

"Damn. Carmen's death is really stirring shit up downtown."

"Yeah, something like this is all them uptight, conservative ass, republicans been waiting on. They've been trying to close Shasta down since she first opened."

"They don't give a fuck that we just lost a friend," said Valerie.

"Naw they don't, they been sending people in left and right 'bout one thing or the other. Thank God Mauy was off last night when they raided us."

"The last thing we need is for the news headline to read, *Unlicensed and Underage Girls Working At Luxury!*"

"Tell me about it," replied Valerie, quickly feeling better than she did before she heard the news. Thinking to herself about how they just keep throwing shit in her lap.

"Damn, I thought Mauy was twenty-one?" stated Valerie.

"Naw, she's eighteen. You, me and Shasta are the only ones that know. I moved her to the day shift and keep her fully dressed just to be on the safe side, since 12 only seem to raid us at night since we been back open."

"I don't have to tell you not to say nothing; right?" asked Stacey.

"Girl, you ain't gotta worry about me saying anything. Me and Mauy cool," said Valerie, lying her ass off.

Truth is, Valerie didn't give a fuck 'bout none of them, and unbeknownst to Stacey, the information she just gave would only add to the chaos Valerie had already caused for Shasta.

"Well love, I would to keep this conversation going, but as you see, it's been hectic around here and I have so much shit to get caught up on," said Stacey.

"Ok. I'll see you later, I'm finna go holler at Shasta anyway," said Valerie.

Valerie went upstairs to Shasta's office. Big Mo was standing out front, she heard him tell Shasta over the walkie talkie, letting her no she was headed her way.

"What up Big Mo?" asked Valerie.

"Shit, same ol', same ol'," replied Big Mo.

Big Mo opened the door for Valerie. When she walked in she saw Mauy sitting on the couch. Valerie went and sat right next to her just to fuck with her.

"How you doing?" asked Valerie.

"We haven't talked in a while. I called a couple times to check on you."

"I know. I'm just getting back out into the world, I was gone get at you."

"It's okay," said Valerie.

"Anyway, I'm good for what it's worth," replied Shasta.

"That's what's up."

Feeling extremely uncomfortable, Mauy got up off the sofa.

"I'm going to get me ah drink. You want something Shasta?" asked Mauy.

"Are you sure you should be drinking?" asked Valerie staring at Mauy.

Mauy ignored Valerie. Shasta didn't pay Valerie's statement any mind either, she had so much others shit on her mind she just didn't think anything of it.

"Shasta? Did you hear me?" asked Mauy with her back turned to Valerie.

"No love. What you say?" asked Shasta.

"I asked if you wanted a drink."

"Naw, I'm good," replied Shasta.

"Okay." said Mauy as she left out the office completely ignoring the fact Valerie was cutting her eyes at her.

"I thought you wasn't coming back until Friday."

"I wasn't, but with Carmen and my clubs being blasted all over the six o'clock news, I had to get out the house," Shasta replied.

"They said on the news this morning that they found an

TWO TIMES BETRAYED

unidentified fingerprint, and that their issuing subpoenas for your employee records."

"That's true. I told them they ain't have to do all that, they could've easily asked me and I would have given them what they needed."

"Fuck. I wanna know what happened to Carmen just as bad as they do. Matter of fact, I got Stacey getting Phase 1 employee information together now as we speak."

Valerie got nervous because she was a Phase 1 employee, and she knew that it wouldn't be long before they got to her. She knew that if Shasta found out who she really was, she could forget revenge. She would have to leave town. Valerie pulled herself together before Shasta noticed the nervousness in her face. She had to find some kinda way to get out of being fingerprinted, and fast.

"I seriously don't wanna talk about this shit anymore," said Shasta.

"Oh, I'm sorry. I know this shit has taken its toll on you."

"You good," said Shasta.

Shasta looked at the schedule to see who all was working tonight and didn't see Valerie's name on it.

"Anyway, what you doing here?" asked Shasta. You finally accept a day off, and you decide to come in anyway?"

"What can I say, you can't keep me away from here," laughs Valerie.

"I used to be the same way back in the day," smiled Shasta.

Valerie looked over to Shasta's cameras and saw Mauy was posted up in Stacey's office now. They looked like they were in deep conversation. Shasta's phone rings and it's Mark calling.

"Sorry love, I gotta take this," said Shasta, giving Valerie her queue to give her some privacy.

"Cool, Imma go back downstairs and fuck with Stacey," said Valerie.

Shasta waves Valerie goodbye and answers her phone for Mark.

"Hey, baby girl. How you holding up?" asked Mark.

"I'm straight," said Shasta.

Mark could hear in her response that she was tired of people

Lynise

asking her that question.

"I was just calling to let you know…"

"Before you finish that statement, Imma call you from another phone."

"Aiight."

Seconds later, Shasta dials Mark back on a burner. He picks up on the first ring.

"Now what you was saying?" asked Shasta.

"I found out where Nico been laying up at," said Mark.

"Where?"

"He renting a spot in Jersey with some Latino bitch."

"Well, go get him!" yelled Shasta, hitting her desk.

"It ain't dat simple. The condos he staying in got high-end security. The only way you getting in there is if you live there or been invited. Point blank. Period," replied Mark.

"I still don't see what's the hold up. Move in that bitch then," said Shasta, growing more frustrated as the conversation went on.

"Love. Calm down. I'm already on that. I gotta appointment with one the realtors Monday. I told you I'm gone see about the nigga and I meant it."

"Yeah, yeah you right. I'm just so fucking pissed off 'bout this shit. On top of Vice raiding my clubs every other fucking night. This shit just keep happening back to back."

"It's all gone be over with soon, and everything gone go back to the basics," said Mark.

"I doubt that shit. I may have to shut my shit down."

"Why you say that?" asked Mark.

"They wanna fingerprint my employee's and my membership list. I don't give a fuck 'bout employees being fingerprinted, but my membership list…that's bad for business; the reason why my clubs are so successful is because of the privacy I offer. If I don't cooperate, it makes matters worse. If I do, my VIP's are going to start canceling their memberships. I don't know what the fuck to do, on top of that shit, if I close down...where in the fuck am I gone get eight million dollars to pay back Mr. Delowe? He ain't going for that *business went bad* shit. Point. Blank. Period."

"Damn. I ain't know they were fucking with you like that," said Mark.

"Well, they are," replied Shasta.

"Let's just handle this shit one issue at a time. I know some people who will smooth Mr. Delowe over if shit hits the fan, but we ain't gotta cross dat bridge yet. What your lawyers talking like?" asked Mark.

"Shit, they say I ain't gotta give em nothing, but at the same time, I don't need 12 posted up in front of my no more than they already is."

"Just to make matters even more crazy, there is no proof that Nico every fought Carmen, plus he had an alibi for the night she was killed, so that domestic dispute shit is out the door."

"Get the fuck outa here. I know there's got to be some kind of report of him beating her ass," said Mark.

"Won't hold up in court. Carmen never called the police on him and when the neighbors did, she denied the fighting. It's like it never happened," said Shasta.

"Okay. Okay. Who is his Alibi?" asked Mark.

"They won't say."

"I'll find out. I wouldn't be surprised if it's the bitch he laying up with now," said Mark.

"Okay."

"Imma hit you up tomorrow. I got you," said Mark.

They both hung the phone. Shasta called Stacey's line because she saw that Mauy was still in her office.

"What up?" asked Stacey.

"Tell Mauy to send dat drink up," replied Shasta.

"What you drinking?" asked Stacey.

"Melody's Special. A big one," said Shasta.

"Okay."

Lynise

A few minutes later, Mauy was in Shasta's office with her drink in hand.

CHAPTER 16

When It Rain, It Pours

Shasta awoke this morning feeling better than she had in weeks. All thanks to the media who were now focusing their attention on a pervert rapist who stalks his victims after assaulting them. Ariel even called a few days ago to let her know the media vans that were usually camped out front were gone. Vice stopped the random raids which everyone in the clubs knew was just their way of seeing free pussy.

Mr. Delove wasn't threatening to pull out his money anymore; shit was finally getting back to normal. So normal that Shasta was able to take a few days off from the club and just relax. At least that's what she thought. Little did she know, shit was about to hit the fan. Before Shasta could get outta bed good, she noticed three missed calls from Stacey. Suddenly the knots started to fill her stomach.

"This can't be good," said Shasta out loud to herself

Stacey had never called before this early in the morning. Shasta unlocked her phone to call Stacey back, but Stacey was calling her back at the same time.

"What's wrong now?" asked Shasta nervously.

"Turn on your T.V." said Stacey.

Shasta grabbed the remote off of the nightstand. Breaking News covered the screen. Shasta almost dropped the phone as she read the

Lynise

headlines and began listening to the reporter.

"We've just received news that the identity of the black male found behind infamous Club Luxury Phase 2 has been identified as Nicholas Horton. The fiancé of Carmen James who was found beaten to death in her apartment several weeks ago. The police are not revealing the cause of death at this time, however my sources tell me that this was a revenge killing. It has been rumored that Nicholas Horton was responsible for Carmen James brutal murder," the reporter announced.

Shasta immediately hung up the phone on Stacey and called Mark. Like clockwork, he answered on the first ring. He couldn't even get his hello out before Shasta started screaming through the phone.

"Have you lost your fucking mind!" yelled Shasta. "You had him killed behind my got damn club!"

"Had who killed? Shasta what the fuck you talking 'bout?" asked Mark, now fully awake and alert as if he was never asleep.

"Now is not the time to be playing fucking games with me Mark. I'm talking about Nico!" yelled Shasta. "They found his fucking body behind my got damn club this morning!" yelled Shasta again.

Mark got outta bed and went into the bathroom. He didn't want the bitch he brought home last night to hear his conversation.

"Whoa, whoa, whoa. Calm down, I ain't have shit to do with that. I'm not fucking stupid, I wouldn't off the nigga at your spot, Shasta," said Mark. "Who told you that?" asked Mark.

"The fucking news is who told me! It's on every got damn channel!" yelled Shasta.

Mark rushed to his living room and turned the T.V. on. On just about every news channel they were showing Nico being lifted in a body bag and Shasta's club on blast in the background.

"Fuck. I swear it wasn't me. I swear!" said Mark.

"I can't believe this shit is happening to me! Shit just started dying down; 12 just stopped harassing me 'bout Carmen and now this shit. I ain't gone never get them muthafuckas to leave me alone now!"

said Shasta.

Shasta heard her phone beep. It was Ariel trying to get through on the other line.

"Hold on, this my other line," said Shasta.

"Yeah," said Mark.

Shasta clicked over.

"They back outside again, and it's a shit load of them," said Ariel, skipping past the usual hey how you doings.

"I know," said Shasta.

"Doll, what's going on now?" asked Ariel.

"I don't know. The news says they found the body of Carmen's ex behind my club early this morning."

"Ain't that the one who you say killed her?" asked Ariel.

"Yeah."

"My God, girl. When it rains it pours. Do you need anything?" asked Ariel.

"Shit, if you can erase the last month of my life so I can start over…that would do me just fine," replied Shasta.

"I wish I could. God knows I wish I could."

"I got someone on the other line. Imma call you back okay."

"Okay, baby doll."

Shasta clicked back over to Mark.

"My bad."

"You good."

"The media already camped out front," said Shasta feeling worse than she did before.

"I'm on my way to come get you. I got a duck off in Philly, you can chill up there for a couple days. At least until I hit da streets to find out what's going on," said Mark.

Shasta lets out a long sigh.

"Aiight."

Shasta's line begins beeping again. This time is was her attorney.

"I gotta go, this is my lawyer calling," said Shasta.

"Imma see you when you get here."

"Aiight, give me 'bout an hour. I gotta make a stop first," said Mark.

"K."

Shasta clicked over and went through her next options with her attorney—which weren't any in her eyes. She didn't want to make any statement and she damn sure wasn't agreeing to the search of her house. They had probable cause for the club, but not for her house. Shasta informed her lawyer she was leaving town for a couple of days. He advised her to stop by his office before she left so that the police could question her. He didn't want the police leaking to the media that she was refusing to cooperate with investigation.

Mark was in her driveway in less than an hour. Shasta had a *ready whenever* bag already packed in her closet. She went into Lil' Chris' room and grabbed his lucky bear, hoping it would bring some kind of luck to her. She met Mark on the porch with her bag in hand.

"You got everything?" asked Mark, grabbing Shasta's bag for her.

"Yeah," said Shasta.

"I gotta stop by my attorney's office before we leave. The police wanna ask me some questions."

"Okay. In the meantime put these on, the media stupid thick out front," said Mark before giving her a pair of D&G sunglasses.

"I know they are."

"It's ridiculous, if it ain't one thing it's another," said Shasta as she got in the car.

"Where is your lawyer's office?" asked Mark.

"Downtown."

"Okay, put your seat belt on."

Once Shasta was strapped in, Mark punched it, flying straight past the camera crew. The tent from Mark's Ferrari kept them from getting any pictures. The only picture they were able to get was of the car, and considering how fast he was going, they barely got that.

CHAPTER 17

Suspicion Is A Bitch

A high profile case is what the media was making it all out to be. Broadcast after broadcast, they were viciously painting Shasta's club as some sort of death pool, even though Carmen was killed at home.

The Medical Examiner held a press conference revealing the results of Nicholas Horton's autopsy report. She announced to the public that Nico died from cardiac arrest due to high levels of cyanide poison and the date rape drug, Molly.

Once again, the police had no witnesses or even a clue as to who would have done this, at the same time, everyone affiliated with Shasta's club was a suspect. That much they made known. They conducted several interviews with Carmen's family and club staff, but was still clueless on what happened. No one was talking. All the police had for evidence was two empty vials they assumed the drugs came in and smudged fingerprints.

Monica, on the other hand, was enjoying every bit of Shasta's misfortunes. Since she couldn't get Vice to shut Shasta's club down for employing underage unlicensed dancers, she took another route and tricked Nico into coming to the club. Nico wasn't hard to manipulate either, just like the average nigga—they let pussy get 'em caught up every time.

Lynise

Monica approached Nico a few days back at his place of business. He owned at least three or four towing services, so she played on his arrogance. She walked in his shop one day, as fine as she was, it wasn't hard for her to seduce him. After she sucked and fucked him, she told him that the nigga who killed his bitch work security at Luxury. They exchanged information and a few days later he was being escorted by Monica to Shasta's Club. She walked him straight through the front entrance. No one noticed or gave him a second look. One thing led to another, and that nother lead to Nico's ass being high and dead as hell behind Shasta's Club.

The media was not letting up 'bout this shit no time soon.

"It done turnt up now, it's time to get this shit rolling in fast gear," Monica said, talking to her T.V.

She grabbed the last four vials of Cyanide poison off her bedroom nightstand and placed them in her handbag. Monica quickly got dressed and headed straight for the club. A week had passed since Nico's death and although Shasta had closed her clubs down for the second time, she still had Stacey arranging meetings between her and the rest of the staff. Monica was excited as ever, due to all the chaos she had caused the previous week before, and she was one of the first employees to arrive to the club, outside of Mauy.

"What's up, honey?" said Valerie to Big Mo as she entered the club.

Valerie was greeted by Stacey as soon as she came in. Shortly thereafter, the rest of the crew started arriving just in the time for the meeting.

"We are having the meeting in the back," said Stacey, looking a nervous wreck.

"Aiight," replied Valerie.

Valerie made her way to the dressing rooms and the rest of the crew followed. She looked over and saw Mauy posted up, as usual, right next to Shasta. Valerie walked directly over toward Mauy. Ironically, Mauy had a new found confidence as well; she reached over and

TWO TIMES BETRAYED

whispered into Valerie's ear.

"Bitch, you ain't fooling me, I know something ain't right 'bout yo' ass. I know you got your hands in a lot of this bullshit going on around here. I can't put my fingers on it right now, but what's done in the dark will come to the light. Trust that. Imma be watching your ass, and just to let you know…I ain't never scared," said Mauy.

Valerie backed up from her, grabbed Mauy's drink out of her hand and sipped it like it was hers. Valerie then leaned back in smiling before giving her response.

"Lil girl, it's best you stay in your lane. With everything that's going on, I'd hate it if something happened to you too," replied Valerie as she walked away.

Moments later, Shasta was calling the meeting to order. Valerie and Mauy were standing on opposite sides of the room, secretly cutting their eyes at each other. It was clear that Mauy grew a back bone over the last couple weeks. Hell, with everything that's been going on, who could help but be in defense mode.

"We all know shit been real crazy around here," Shasta stated. "However, we ain't gone let this minor shit throw us off. Stacey is passing around confidentiality agreements for you all to sign. I expect signatures from all of you; if you can't comply…it was nice working with you. Stacey will also get at y'all to let y'all know when we'll be opening back up. Until then, take a vacation," said Shasta adjourning the meeting.

Valerie sat back and watched the entire staff sign their agreement contracts. She was the last to give her signature. Mark sat back in the cut and kept his eyes on Shasta the whole time. He had a strong feeling to protect her now.

"I gotta do one last walk through before we head out," said Shasta, talking to Mark.

"Aiight," replied Mark.

Shasta left everyone and headed for her office. She knew it wouldn't be long before 12 was back with another search warrant.

Lynise

Only this time, her lawyer made sure she'd be ready for them. They could look through anything they wanted, but they would not have access to her membership list and her employees could not discuss them. She took the 40K and the contract she had with Mr. Delowe out of the safe. She went to snatch up her laptop and saw an email in her personal account flashing across the screen from a Cybercam1908. Curious since only a hand full of people had her personal email address, she sat down and clicked it open.

"This better not be spam," said Shasta out loud to herself.

The subject line of the email read in big bold letters: WARNING! Shasta continued to read as follows:

"*Greetings,*

Imma get straight to the point due to the shitload of chaos you're involved in. I thought now would be a good time to make you aware of your DEADLY surroundings. However, my information comes with a hefty price tag. But I'm sure you can accommodate. My fee for this knowledge is 100K and to convince you of how much my knowledge would mean to you, here's a little mental note for you: The once before Shasta Smithson now known as Shasta Davis had to change her name and relocate to Connecticut because of what happened back in Miami two years ago. Kila is dead. Jason is dead. Black is dead. Big is dead, and let's not forget your son's father, Big Chris. Should I go on?

Sincerely,

Your new business partner"

Shasta almost fell out of her chair. All she could think of was, *who is this nigga, and how in the fuck did he know all this*. What happened in Miami didn't even get News play because nobody was giving a fuck about a dead stripper and drug dealers.

Stacey entered her office holding the signed agreements in her hand. Shasta immediately brushed her off.

"Not right now!" yelled Shasta.

Without a question, Stacey turned around and left. Mauy flew past

Stacey on the way to Shasta's office as well. She was so dead set on telling her about Valerie that she didn't hear Stacey trying to tell her that now wasn't a good time to be trying to go in there. Mauy bursts into Shasta's office as she always did and got the business too.

"I got something to tell you!" said Mauy.

"Got damn it! Not now! Get the fuck out my office!" yelled Shasta.

Mauy did the same as Stacey and immediately left Shasta's office without saying another word. Stacey was sitting at the bar having a drink with Melody when she saw Mauy come back down from Shasta's office. By the expression on Mauy's face, Stacey could tell Shasta snapped on her as well. Mauy walked over and pulled a seat up next to Stacey at the bar.

"What's wrong with Shasta?" asked Mauy.

Stacey shrugged her shoulders.

"That's a stupid question. With all this shit happening to her back to back, on top of losing money every day the club is closed…you would be a lil snappy too," Melody offered.

"Yeah, you right," replied Mauy.

"What you wanted with her anyway?" asked Stacey.

"I was trying to tell her about Valerie," Mauy replied.

"What about her?" asked Stacey.

"I've been watching her ass lately. For real, for real y'all, something ain't right 'bout dat bitch. She doesn't seem to care 'bout none of the shit that's been going on around here, and when Shasta was holding the meeting, I coulda swore I saw her smiling, when Shasta was talking 'bout what's been happening. Like she was happy shit was fucked up," stated Mauy.

"That's what you was rushing upstairs to tell her?" asked Melody.

"Yeah," Mauy said with confidence.

"Really? Just because a person handle stress differently from other people doesn't mean they up to something," said Stacey.

"You forget Carmen said the same shit 'bout yo' ass," said Melody.

"That was different. I know that bitch is up to something. I can feel it in my gut!" stated Mauy.

"Well, feel this…" said Melody as she gave Mauy a drink to calm her ass down because she was getting a little too excited.

"Look honey, Shasta got enough bullshit on her plate. The last thing she wanna hear is female drama," Stacey warned.

"I know right. Do us all a favor and let that shit go," said Melody.

Before Mauy could say another word, Valerie was joining them at the bar.

"What's up ladies?" asked Valerie.

She had been watching them from across the room the whole time. They were so busy listening to Mauy, they hadn't even noticed her. She could tell from Mauy's body language, that she didn't like what Mauy was telling them.

"Hey, girl," said Melody, completely brushing Mauy's comments off.

"What y'all drinking?" asked Valerie.

"Melody's Special."

"You want one?" asked Melody.

"Of course. I could use a drink right now."

"Make me another one too," said Stacey.

"How about you?" asked Melody.

"Naw, I'm good," replied Mauy as she walked off.

Valerie could tell that coming to join them at the bar had pissed Mauy off.

"Is she okay?" asked Valerie, knowing that she really didn't give a fuck.

"Girl, pay her no mind, it's something wrong with her every other week," said Melody.

"She good, she just young as hell and take everything to heart," said Valerie.

"She will grow out of it once she experiences a little more life. We all was like that at one point in our lives," said Stacey to Mauy's defense.

TWO TIMES BETRAYED

The ladies nodded in agreement.

Meanwhile, back in the office, Shasta pulled herself together and responded to Cybercam1908 email via chat.

Shasta typed: *Who the fuck is you?*

Ten minutes passed before Cybercam1908 replied.

It read: *I'm the way of light through your darkness.*

Shasta typed: *Well, bitch shine bright. I ain't got time for the games. What do you have to tell me?*

Cybercam1908 typed: *Nor do I find the playing of games amusing. As I mentioned earlier, there is a fee for services. This rotten apple you have in your circle is out to do you PERMANENT harm. Knowing your background Ms. Davis, I felt this was something you would be interested in learning.*

Shasta poured herself the last of the vodka she kept in her desk.

The chat screen blinked: Cybercam1908 is typing…

It read: *Think it over. You can wire the 100K to this account 00691863400 rte# 066.192.664. I hope you come to a decision before it's too late.*

Cybercam1908 signed off.

Shasta sat at her desk mad as fuck, just about ready to throw her laptop across the room. She had all this shit going at the club, now some muthafucka she don't know trying to extort her. Feelings aside, she couldn't help but think there was truth to what Cybercam1908 was claiming. She had been down this road before and really couldn't afford to risk it. She also knew than no one in Connecticut knew about Miami but her and Mark. She was watching him chat it up with Big Mo during the time she was going back and forth with Cybercam1908, so she knew he wasn't on some slick shit. She immediately called Mark into her office. He could hear the panic in her voice. Mark walked in and saw that something was wrong.

"Someone else knows about Miami."

Mark sat down preparing himself for what he was about to hear next.

G STREET CHRONICLES
A LITERARY POWERHOUSE
WWW.GSTREETCHRONICLES.COM

Chapter 18

The Cat Is Out The Bag Now

Shasta sat quietly for a second before she informed Mark what just happened. Staring at her cameras, she saw a white cable van parked out front. It was obviously 12, but she didn't give a fuck though…she had other shit going on now.

"So what's up? How you know somebody else knows about Miami? What happened?" asked Mark.

Shasta turned her laptop around for Mark to read the email and chats between her and Cybercam1908. The more he read, the more he shook his head in disbelief.

"Fuck. Shit just won't let up for you, baby girl," said Mark.

"Tell me about it."

"Who you think it could be?" asked Mark.

"I don't fucking know!" yelled Shasta.

Mark pulled the blunt of Loud from behind his ear and lit it.

"Do you think I should pay him?" asked Shasta.

Choking, Mark passed the blunt to Shasta before he answered her.

"You got the facts, it's clear the nigga know what he talking about. Me personally, if I was you I'd shoot him the lil check. Only because of what you went through with Kila, and we both know firsthand how sour that shit went. You can't afford to have another one of her in your circle. 100K won't fuck your pockets up in the least bit, even if

Lynise

it's some bullshit," said Mark.

Hitting the blunt again before she passed it back, Shasta nodded her head in agreement.

"I feel the same way."

"Fuck it. What I got to lose?" said Shasta.

Mark reached in his pocket and pulled out his wallet to give Shasta his Black Card.

"I got the 100K for you," said Mark.

Shasta gave Mark a real confused look while reaching in her handbag to get her own Black Card out. Mark took it from her. She could tell he was serious.

"I said I got you, now tell me what you need me to do," stated Mark.

Shasta wrote the account information on a sticky note and passed it to Mark.

"Aiight," he said. He dialed his accountant and twenty minutes later funds were transferred to Cybercam1908's account.

"It's done."

"Okay," said Shasta.

They both sat back and waited. This had to be the longest fifteen minutes in both of their lives. Cybercam1908 emailed Shasta minutes after the money posted to his account. Shasta opened the email and saw a huge picture of Big and his wife Monica. Her mouth dropped. She couldn't believe what she was seeing. The Monica she once knew was now the woman she now knew as Valerie.

"You got to be fucking kidding me!"

"What?" asked Mark curiously.

"That bitch Valerie is fucking Monica!" yelled Shasta.

Still looking lost and confused, Mark got up and walked around Shasta's desk to see what she was looking at on her laptop. Immediately recognizing the picture, Mark headed straight for the door. They both knew Monica was still in the club because they had her in eye view on the camera still sitting at the bar with Melody and Stacey.

TWO TIMES BETRAYED

"Aye!" yelled Shasta, stopping Mark before he left out her office. "What a minute. He's typing me something via chat."

Mark came back around to see what Cybercam1908 was typing.

It read: *I take it the information I provided did you some justice. I also wanted to let you know that I sold her five vials of Cyanide 200mg. I felt obligated to tell you what Ms. Thang had planned for you after doing my research on what happened in Miami. It became clear to me that she was taking her revenge out on the wrong person. The cause of her problem was already dead. Plus, it gave me a chance to make a few extra bucks.*

Shasta responded back to his chat, feeling truly better about life. She had a smile from ear to ear.

It read: *A few extra bucks my ass, lol. I can imagine how much you hit her for, but it's cool. No stress.*

Cybercam1908 typed: *Any who...young lady, I would love to chat more, but unfortunately, I have money to spend. You be careful and if you need me in the future, I'm an email away.*

Shasta typed: *Of course. I'll keep in touch. Thank you.*

Cybercam1908 typed: *My pleasure.*

Cybercam1908 logged off.

Pacing the floor, Shasta could tell Mark was getting more angry by the minute.

"Love, calm down. I got something for that bitch," said Shasta.

"Fuck that!" said Mark, grabbing his strap and staring at the camera.

"For real, for real...this bitch thinks she got me thrown in the blender. I want her to keep thinking she got the ups."

"You know what? You right, that bitch won't even see it coming," said Mark.

"My point. Trust me when I say I got something for that bitch," said Shasta.

"Sooner than later this go round," replied Mark.

Shasta sat back in her chair with a million thoughts going through her head at the same damn time. She paged Melody and had her send

Lynise

Mauy upstairs with a bottle of Remy. A few minutes later, Mauy was walking through the door with the bottle. Mark was still slick amped up; Shasta hurriedly and poured him a drink.

"We gone need taller glasses," said Shasta, sending Mauy back downstairs for the taller glasses.

Melody had the glasses on the counter waiting for Mauy when she came back downstairs. Valerie had left to use the restroom.

"Thanks," said Mauy, picking up the glasses and heading back upstairs to Shasta's office.

Mauy placed the new glasses on the table and grabbed the other ones to take back to the bar.

Not knowing the intercom was still on, Shasta poured her and Mark a drink.

"Calm down. We celebrating!" said Shasta with happiness in her voice.

"Celebrating fucking what?" asked Stacey. "All this shit's fucked up around here," stated Stacey a lil tipsy.

"Oops," said Shasta, laughing at Stacey's comment.

"Cheer up love, it's gone be alright," said Shasta talking to Stacey before she switched the intercom off.

Shasta sat at her desk in pure satisfaction. Mark was relaxed and she could tell he had his thinking cap on now. For the first time in months, she wasn't concerned about the outcome of anything because the ball was finally in her court. For the first time in months, she was actually stress free. She turned around and started playing "No Worries" by Lil' Wayne. Once again, she was back in control of things; she knew who the problem was, and by all means, she was going to solve it. Point. Blank. Period.

Chapter 19

Problem Solved

"The old saying still applies. Watch your friends, and your enemies closer."
-HOODNOMICS

The sun rose a little brighter this morning with all the latest news still plaguing her mind. Shasta awoke to Stacey, Mark, Valerie, Big Mo and Mauy stretched across her couture sofa and cashmere rug half naked. Wiping the cold out her eyes, she sat up fully in her chair to better observe the slumber party that took place last night. Searching for her shit, she didn't even remember falling asleep. Barely awake herself, she tapped Stacey trying to wake her ass up too. Still tapping Stacey, Shasta watched as she tossed and turned in disturbance of her so delicate looking sleep.

"Girl. Get yo' ass up!" said Shasta smacking her hardly on the ass.

Stacey jumped up, looking in space. It took her a few minutes before she realized where she was.

"What the fuck went on in here last night?" asked Stacey, immediately recognizing her bra on the floor beside her. "And how in the fuck I end up on the floor?"

"Fuck if I know," replied Shasta.

"Ask Molly?"

Stacey burst out laughing.

"From the looks of it, we had fun," said Stacey, grabbing the rest of her clothes.

"It's always fun when you fucking with me," replied Shasta.

"Yeah, so much damn fun you don't remember shit till we watch it on your cameras. Imma pass this time. I don't wanna see nothing. If it was meant for me to remember. I would have," said Stacey with a slight grin.

Shasta nodded her head in agreement with Stacey.

"I don't wanna see a mistake I coulda made either," replied Stacey staring at Big Mo. "Eww," Stacey said before reaching for the blunt of Kush out of the astray.

They sat for a good lil minute in silence smoking, still watching everyone else sleep. Shasta gestured for Stacey to follow her outside her office. She had her index finger over her mouth, letting her know to exit quietly. Stacey looked at Shasta with curiosity, trying to figure out why they were sneaking out the office instead of her waking everyone up and putting they ass out.

"Why da hell we creeping out yo' office?" asked Stacey.

"Cause, I wanna put you up on some shit."

"What?" asked Stacey in a more serious tone.

"Let's go get some food, I'll tell you in a minute."

"Aiight."

Stacey readjusted her clothes to make sure she wasn't looking like a women of the night.

"Girl, you straight," said Shasta, noticing what she was doing.

"Un, huh."

A few minutes later, they were pulling up in front of the Waffle House 'bout two blocks away from the club.

"So what you got to put me up on?" asked Stacey anxiously wanting to know.

Shasta put her truck in park, switched off the engine and turned toward Stacey, giving her her full attention. The expression on her face made it clear to Stacey that this wasn't going to be regular type chit chat.

TWO TIMES BETRAYED

"I don't like the way you looking."

"I don't think I can take anymore fucked up news," said Stacey, lighting a cigarette.

"Man, damn. You gone let me tell you or what?"

Stacey nodded.

"Okay, so to make a long story short. The bitch Valerie is really this hoe named Monica from Atlanta. I had her nigga knocked off after a jug me—and my used to be—dead ass best friend pulled that went all the way sour," said Shasta.

Stacey sat there with her mouth wide open. She never pictured Shasta as some gangster bitch. A part of her knew Shasta had to at least have been a stripper before, but that was only because she was too good at operating her club.

"Damn."

"Mauy kept trying to tell me something wasn't right about her, but I just kept brushing her off, thinking it was just the usual bitch shit these broads normally go through around here," said Stacey.

"Yeah, me too. I remember Mauy tried to come to me a few months back. I ain't pay the shit no attention either."

"So what the move is?" asked Stacey.

"Shit you already know…Imma see about that bitch."

"Come to find out, she been going back and forth with some internet nigga. That's how she found me. Irony of that shit, that same nigga is who put me up on her dumb ass," replied Shasta.

"Get the fuck outta here?" Stacey couldn't believe her ears.

"Yeah. The shit had me thowed at first too," said Shasta.

"Who else knows who the bitch really is?"

"Mark. Soon as he saw the email, he wanted to put a bullet in her head."

"You shoulda let him," replied Stacey.

"As bad as I wanted to dat would have been stupid though, with all this shit that's been going on, the last thing I need is a dead bitch with her head blown off in my got damn club," replied Shasta.

Lynise

"Yeah, you right, but I hope you talking 'bout seeing 'bout that bitch sooner than later."

"Trust that I got something for that bitch; da internet nigga say he sold her some Cyanide—that instant death shit. I take it that bitch planned on using that shit on me."

Face frowned up, Stacey looked at Shasta like *bitch we can go see 'bout her ass now*. She reached in her handbag and grabbed another cigarette.

"Whatever you need luv, just let me know. You know I got your back," said Stacey.

"Yeah, I know."

About an hour later, they were back in Shasta's office—food in hand and the room filled with smoke and laughter. Mark looked at Shasta, remembering the news from the night before. Although last night Molly had his dick in Valerie's mouth, that still didn't change the fact that he wanted to blast her ass for Shasta. He kept his composure. Shasta winked at him, letting him know she knew what he was thinking.

"Well, this was fun; even though I can barely remember shit," said Big Mo.

"I gotta go before I end up fucking divorced."

"Hell yeah, we all know dat shit. Keisha 'bout three minutes away from pulling up and fucking your ass up," said Valerie.

They all laughed and all their laughs were fake as fuck.

"Well huh," said Stacey, passing Big Mo the bag of food.

"At least if you gone get the business, yo' ass can be full."

Downing the chicken sandwich like his ass ain't ate in days, Big Mo grabbed his pistol off of the table and headed for the door.

"Nigga yo' ass better run," said Shasta, still teasing Big Mo.

"Ha, ha, I see y'all ass got jokes," replied Big Mo, throwing his middle finger up behind him as he left.

"Bye!" laughed Mauy at how fast he was getting down the steps.

Stacey went to Shasta's little refrigerator and pulled out two bottles of champagne.

TWO TIMES BETRAYED

"Ooh! What's the occasion?" asked Valerie.

Mauy interrupted.

"Shit new beginnings, luv."

Valerie smirked at Mauy, really not caring about shit she had to say.

"I can dig it," replied Valerie.

Still half naked, Valerie reached for her handbag to grab her makeup. She had no clue that they all knew who she really was and what she had planned. They all played it real G, kicking it like any other day.

Stacey gave each of them a flute and Mauy initiated the toast.

"Attention, attention…" said Mauy, tapping her glass with one of the waffle house forks. "I just want to say that I love you all. You guys are like family to me, especially you," said Mauy, looking directly at Shasta.

"Ahh, we love you too," they replied.

"And last, but not least, loyalty means everything," said Mauy with her attention turned to Valerie now.

"Here!" said Stacey.

"Here, here!" said Mark and Shasta.

Valerie finished getting dressed and continued to small talk with Stacey. Shasta refilled all of their glasses. She purposely placed her flute by Valerie's, she had a gut feeling that the bitch was going to try some shit. She also knew that she had the vials on her. Shasta wasn't about to let Valerie out of her sight. Today was the day. She winked at Stacey, giving her the queue to get everyone out of the room expect her and Valerie. Holding her hands between her legs, Mauy set it in motion.

"This is the only thing I hate about drinking," said Mauy pacing back and forth, trying to keep from using the restroom on herself.

"Let me guess…you gotta pee?" asked Stacey.

"Hell yeah," replied Mauy.

"Then go! It looks like you 'bout to piss on yourself."

"Damn it, I gotta piss too," said Mark.

Lynise

"This should be interesting. I wonder who gone make it to the restroom first."

Mauy took off running to go use Shasta's private restroom. Mark was right behind her.

"Somebody gone be using the sink…watch," said Stacey, following right behind them.

"Y'all nasty. I better not smell piss in my sink!" said Shasta, knowing that that was the excuse to get her and Valerie alone.

Soon as Shasta turned her back, Valerie hurriedly emptied two vials of cyanide into Shasta's flute. She was so anxious to fuck Shasta up, she didn't know Shasta saw her and had already switched flutes. Instead, she went along with it, kicking it like she was fucked up. Shasta picked up her glass and walked toward Valerie.

"Let's make our own toast," said Shasta, slurring her words a little.

"Of course," said Valerie, unable to hide the bullshit ass smirk from across her face at this point.

They both held there flutes up.

"Toast to those caught with their pants down."

"Um, okay," said Valerie, looking puzzled for a second. Hatred was all over her face. Valerie could no longer hide her motives at this point. When she saw Shasta drink the last of the champagne, she had a grin on her face that was obvious to anyone looking on that it was some shit in the game. Valerie was confident that she had finally gotten Shasta. She walked over to lock the door. She wanted to watch her die without any interruptions.

"Damn, bae, you cheezing like fuck," said Shasta. "You must have really related to my toast."

"What can I say? It really fit for the moment," replied Valerie with a grin.

Shasta placed the empty flute on her table and sat in her chair. Minutes later, Shasta was looking as Valerie pushed up against the wall trying to keep from falling.

"Shit. I don't feel good," said Valerie.

TWO TIMES BETRAYED

"I know you don't…Monica," said Shasta, making her aware of that she knew who she was.

Monica's eyes slurred as she fell to the floor.

"FUCK YOU!" replied Monica, barley getting her words out.

Shasta walked over toward her and squatted down beside her. She pulled the two empty vials of cyanide out her bra and shoved them in Monica's mouth. "Stupid bitch you liked to got me. I'll give it to you though, you did have me fooled. If it wasn't for your little internet friend putting me up on game, I'd be the one laying here dying now instead of you."

Struggling to breathe, Monica tried her best to get up.

"I don't think so bitch!" said Shasta, kicking Monica in the face and back down to the ground. "Bitch , you got blood on my rug!" said Shasta as she reached over and kicked her again.

"Fuck you bitch. I still left my mark in your life and I took your sweet Carmen with me hoe." said Monica, barely wiping the blood from her face.

"Fuck you!" said Monica, spitting out her last words.

Shasta watched Monica take her last breath. Still mad as fuck, she reached over and slapped her a few times, hoping that it would help the mixture of feelings she was having right now. It didn't, there was no satisfaction in beating on a dead person. Shasta sat on the floor next to Monica's body, she thought of Kila and her son. To move over a 1,000 miles cross country to put the past bullshit behind her just to have it follow her had her fucked up. She couldn't believe how close she came to death this go round.

Mark, Stacey and Mauy banged on the door to her office. She didn't know that Monica had locked them in.

"Yo! Shasta open the door!" yelled Mark.

Before she could get up to open it, Mark was kicking it down. Mauy ran to Shasta's side first. She just stood there next to her in silence holding her hand. Stacey stepped over Monica's body, grabbed the bottle of champagne and turnt it up.

"Fuck!" yelled Stacey.

"What's wrong?" asked Mark.

"Am I drinking that crazy bitch poison?" asked Stacey nervously. Shasta couldn't help but laugh at Stacey.

"Girl, calm down, I wouldn't have let you drink that shit," said Shasta, pointing to vials laid in blood on the rug.

"I need a strong drink," said Stacey, flopping down on the couch.

"Me, too!" replied Shasta.

"I'll go get a bottle of Remy from downstairs," said Mauy.

Mark was still standing in the same spot as if he had never seen a dead bitch before. He was in deep thought trying to figure out what they were going to do with the body now.

"Snap back to life. It was just pussy!" said Mauy, teasing Mark. Shasta just shook her head.

"Psst…whatever. I ain't studying this bitch. I'm trying to figure out what the hell we gone do with this bitch's body," replied Mark.

"Nigga, your ass was stuck for a minute," said Stacey.

"Hell, yeah," laughed Shasta.

"Man, whatever. It's always bitches getting me into shit," said Mark jokingly.

"Yeah, yeah we know you da man. Now can you please get on the phone and call your peeps so y'all can get this parasite out my office," said Shasta.

"I'm doing it now," said Mark going through his contact on his phone

"How about we burn the bitch? Send her ass to hell right along with Nico," said Stacey, finishing the rest of the champagne off.

"Nico in hell alright, but he ain't there for killing Carmen," said Shasta.

"What you mean by that?" asked Mark.

"It was all her. She killed both of them; she knew Nico used to beat on Carmen. She did all that shit to get to me," said Shasta.

"Fucking bitch!" said Stacey.

TWO TIMES BETRAYED

Mark went over and spit on Monica's body.

"I wish we would've found out about her before Carmen got caught up in this shit," said Mark.

"Me too," said Shasta.

The room got silent for a minute as they all sat back and thought of Carmen.

"Shit, I think we should burn the bitch," said Mark.

"Hell, yeah."

Mauy returned with the bottle of Remy and four shot glasses. She sat the glasses on the table and poured everybody up. She also poured some of it on Monica dead ass.

"Wait a minute bitch, that hoe dead; don't waste no liquor on her," said Stacey, a little wasted now.

They all just laughed at her. Mark sat on Shasta's desk and just smiled at all of them.

"Y'all some crazy ass broads for real, for real," said Mark.

Shasta got up and took off all the jewelry Monica had on. Mauy grabbed the scissors and cut off Monica's hair.

"What the hell you cutting the bitch's hair off for?" asked Shasta.

"Cuz, I want the bitch to fry bald and broke."

"She don't need no hair where she going," said Mauy.

They just shook they heads.

"She's the crazy one," said Stacey.

Mark drug Monica's body aside, waiting on the Calvary to come. Mauy went through her handbag and took out the money and handed it to Mark. It was a little over 5k.

"The bitch paying for her own funeral," said Mauy.

"Girl, you hell," laughed Shasta.

"Our little Mauy growing up right before our eyes," said Stacey.

"She sure has come a long way from the day I first hired her ass."

"Y'all done made her into a little gangsta," laughed Mark.

"I know right," said Shasta.

Mauy poured everyone another round while Shasta rolled up a

Lynise

blunt of Loud. Stacey turned on the Boze surround sound to play Shasta's favorite rapper, Young Jeezy. For sure this was one hellafied morning, they all had a bond that would tie them together for the rest of their lives. Completely ignoring the fact that there was a dead body over in the corner, they partied like it was the usual business of the club.

Chapter 20

Goodbye & Hello Love

Two months later, with everything packed and loaded via Good Brothers Moving, Shasta was done with her club ventures. Mr. Delowe decided to buy both clubs from her, totaling over 50 million dollars with the guarantee of Mauy and Stacey remaining employed. He also agreed to keep Big Mo on as well. The media had finally taken the spot light off her and her club due to the fact that they weren't able to link her to anything. Shasta was leaving Connecticut, headed happily back to Atlanta.

Shasta had only a few stops to make before her flight. Of course one of those stops was to Mark's spot. She decided to call him instead of just popping up. He knew she was leaving and going back to Atlanta. She dialed Mark's number. Soon as he sees her picture on his IPhone 5, he answers almost dropping the phone. Mark pushes the random chick out his arms, scooting to the edge of the bed to better hear Shasta.

"What up love?" asked Mark, trying to sound sleepy.

"Nigga, I know you ain't still asleep. What random bitch you brought home last night?" asked Shasta.

"What you talking 'bout? Ain't nobody here with me shawty."

"Nigga, this me you talking to, I know you can't sleep alone."

"For real, for real...no bullshit," said Mark, tapping the chick and

Lynise

signaling her in the direction of the door.

"What the fuck?" stated the girl.

Shasta could hear her in the background even though Mark tried his best to cover the phone.

"Un, huh. So who was that? The dog?" laughed Shasta.

Mark sat in silence, trying to think of something to say. Shasta was the only woman out of all the bitches he fucked with who made him draw a blank. He deeply cared about what she thought of him.

"Newsy nigga, I'm going back home today. I was gone come through and kick it with you for a minute, but I see you have company. So Imma just see you when I see you…lata," said Shasta as she hung the phone up. Mark couldn't get one word out, Shasta was already on the other line calling to say her goodbyes to Ariel. Ariel's son Zack answered.

"Hello," said Zack.

"Hey man. Where is your momma?" asked Shasta.

"She's in the kitchen. It looks like y'all moving. Are y'all moving, Ms. Shasta?" asked Zack.

"Yeah, we are, love."

"But…you can't. Me and my brother wanted to make Lil' Chris our best friend," said Zack sadly.

"Oh, honey…Lil' Chris can still be you guy's best friend."

"How about I bring him back up here to visit for the summer break. Would you and Ryan like that?" asked Shasta.

"Very much so," replied Zack.

Shasta overheard Ariel in the back ground asking Zack who he was on the phone with.

"Ms. Shasta," stated Zack.

"Hey, doll," said Ariel.

"Hey."

"I know darn well you not saying goodbye to me over the phone," said Ariel.

"I'm not good with goodbye's honey."

TWO TIMES BETRAYED

"Bullshit. I'm walking over there now," said Ariel as she hung up the phone.

Shasta met Ariel and the boys outside. Zack and Ryan ran up to hug her and gave her another hug for Lil' Chris.

"I wish we could've told Lil' Chris goodbye," said Ryan.

"Me too," replied Shasta.

"Y'all gone now and play. Let me and Ms. Shasta talk," said Ariel, directing her boys to go back home.

They both said okay and ran off. Shasta could feel her phone vibrating in her pocket. When she looked at it, she saw nine missed calls from Mark. She couldn't hide the smile from her face, or from Ariel for that matter.

"Who was that that's got you smiling so big?" asked Ariel.

Shasta didn't say anything.

"Uh, huh, let me guess. It's Mark."

Shasta just stood there blushing from ear to ear.

"I knew you liked him. Why you trying to fight it?" asked Ariel.

"I'm not fighting nothing, we just friends."

"Friends my ass, I said the same thing about the boy's daddy."

"For real Ariel, that's all we are. Nothing more."

"Yeah, whatever."

"How is he taking the move back to Atlanta?" asked Ariel.

"I really don't know. We haven't discussed it, plus, he ain't my man so he should be cool with it."

"I doubt that, doll. Y'all two been stuck together like glue these last few weeks. Have you given him some yet?"

"OH MY GOD! No," said Shasta.

"Well, what you waiting on? You know you got feelings for him," said Ariel.

"No I don't. And I most definitely don't have any time for all his hoes."

"Darling, I gotta feeling he will cut all that nonsense out if you gave him a chance."

Lynise

"So you feeling shit now," laughed Shasta.

"Ha, ha...feeling real deep love coming from you."

"I ain't fucking with Mark girl."

"Yes, you will be. I can see it in your eyes; every time you hear his name your face lights up."

Shasta gave off a sigh. She knew Ariel was right, she did have strong feelings for Mark. She also knew she was wasting her time trying to convince her otherwise.

"What time does your flight leave?" asked Ariel, jumping subjects.

"Later this evening."

"Well, Imma miss you dearly," said Ariel hugging Shasta.

"I'm gone miss you too," said Shasta, starting to tear up.

"You have to go, I told you I don't like goodbyes."

"Me either," said Ariel.

They embarrassed each other once more before Ariel left going back home.

"Stay in touch."

"I will."

Shasta forced back tears as she watched her good friend leave. Still thinking of Mark, she saw that she had missed three more calls from him.

"Let me call this nigga back before he be pulling up," said Shasta out loud to herself.

Most certainly he picked up on the first ring.

"Why the fuck you just now answering my calls?" asked Mark.

"Nigga, calm down. I just saw that you called."

"You still coming by the house?" asked Mark.

"You still want me too?" asked Shasta.

"Hell, yeah, plus, I got something for you."

"Oh, really?"

"Yeah."

"Okay, well I'm going to stop and get me something to smoke and I'll be on my way."

TWO TIMES BETRAYED

"Just come straight to the shop, I'm on deck," said Mark.

"Which one you at?" asked Shasta.

"Pine."

"Okay."

They both hung up and thirty minutes later Shasta was pulling up outside his shop. She saw the driveway lined up with every bit of thirty huge Gold and Green Balloons, along with Big Mo and Nick standing out front to escort her in. Once she got inside, she couldn't see anything because all the lights were turned off. She started calling for Mark, but he didn't answer. She turned around to try and leave and all she heard was…

"We gone miss you!"

Shasta just stood there smiling. She looked around to see, Mauy, Stacey, Melody and Mark; each of them holding cards and a bottle of champagne. Shasta was very happy to see all of them. Mauy was the first to walk over to her.

"What you thought you was just gone leave and not tell us goodbye," said Mauy.

Shasta grabbed her glass and hugged Mauy tightly.

"I think I'm going to miss you most of all," said Shasta still hugging Mauy.

"Don't make me cry again. I just fixed my makeup."

Stacey and Melody joined them.

"Imma miss your moody ass too," said Stacey, wiping the tears from her eyes.

"Looks like she about to fuck up your Mascara too," said Mauy.

"Shut up," laughed Stacey.

Shasta grabbed Stacey by both hands.

"I'm not dying boo," laughed Shasta.

"Hell, its 'bout time you took your overgrown ass outside of Connecticut anyway."

"Let me know when you're ready and I'll send you a plane ticket. Okay?"

Lynise

"Okay," replied Stacey.

Shasta reached over and pulled Melody closer to her as well.

"Who gone make my Melody's Special now?" asked Shasta.

"No one better than me. That's why you should stay."

"We both know I can't do that," said Shasta.

"I know."

Melody placed her head on Shasta's shoulder.

"Imma miss you."

"Imma miss all of you too."

"When I get settled back home, Imma fly you down."

"Naw, you know I ain't leaving Connecticut. I never have and probably never will."

"Well, I promise to visit soon," said Shasta.

"Okay," said Melody.

Big Mo and Nick were the last to say their goodbyes, all while Mark stood back and watched everyone from afar.

"I ain't with this bye shit," said Big Mo.

"Me either," said Nick.

They grouped hugged her and walked off.

"See y'all later," said Shasta quietly as she watched Big Mo and Nick leave. She knew it would be a while before she saw any of them again.

Shasta took her last sip of champagne, waived her final goodbyes to all of them and left outside the shop with Mark.

"Thank you so much for this, I had no idea on how I was gone tell them all bye," said Shasta.

"You good baby, you ain't have to say nothing. I told you I got you from the jump."

"Yeah, you did."

Shasta and Mark sat outside at the table, watching the last of the crew disappear into traffic.

"I'm really going to miss all of them," said Shasta.

"Me too," said Mark.

TWO TIMES BETRAYED

Shasta looked at him confused.

"What you mean by you *too*?" asked Shasta.

Mark looked Shasta dead in her eyes before he responded.

"I mean I don't wanna say goodbye."

"I wanna start over with you back home in Atlanta," said Mark.

Shasta returned the stare before she got up and went to the other side of the table. Not knowing what to do with the emotions she was feeling, she had to get up from near him.

"No bullshit, No strays, No lies. Just us. I know you know I want your ass girl," said Mark walking toward her.

"Wants and needs are two totally different things Mark; and you gotta know I ain't got time for no new bullshit," replied Shasta.

"I ain't offering bullshit. I'm offering a stress free family."

"Why me?"

"Shasta, to be for real, for real…I've always wanted you, even when you was rocking with Big Chris. It just wasn't our time, so I dipped and set up shop here. When I saw you at your club two years ago, I knew I was going to have you."

Shasta just continued to stare at Mark, not believing what she was hearing.

"What's it gone be?" asked Mark.

"I mean my flight is in less than four hours."

"Don't worry about that. You ain't flying…we driving my truck home," said Mark.

"Our clothes are already packed in my truck."

Shasta could no longer hide her blushing from him. She saw that he was dead ass serious about being with her and she wanted badly to be with him.

"What am I gone do about my Range?" asked Shasta.

"You gave it to Mauy."

"I did?" replied Shasta, noticing her truck was no longer in the parking lot.

"Damn. What if I would have said no and yo' ass done already

Lynise

gave my truck away," laughed Shasta.

"I had faith." replied Mark, holding her hand in his now.

Mark leaned in and kissed Shasta; since everyone was gone, he picked her up and totted her into his office. He slowly undressed her while kissing her from head to toe. Things began to get real heated, Mark pushed the shit off his desk onto the floor, and Shasta submissively complied and accepted his manhood into her. Moan after moan, scream after scream, pound after pound they both found themselves from the desk to the floor. Mark whispered in Shasta's ear.

"Your mine now," said Mark.

"And I ain't sharing."

"You ain't got to."

"Good," replied Shasta.

After about two hours of laying up and talking shit, it was time to go. Mark and Shasta barely got dressed before they were at round two. Shasta staggered to the restroom trying to pull herself together.

"Where's my phone at baby? Matter of fact, did you get my shit out my truck?" asked Shasta.

"Ha, I'm *baby* now, and yes, I had Big Mo take care of that already and your phone is behind you," replied Mark.

Shasta finished getting dressed and grabbed her phone to see that she had a missed call from her sister Candace. Feeling good, she didn't really feel like talking to her sister; she was glad Candace's call had gone to voicemail.

"Be there Sunday, sis," said Shasta.

Mark overheard her and corrected her.

"More like some time Monday."

"Why you say that?" asked Shasta.

"Cuz I ain't nowhere near through with your ass yet."

"Oh, really?"

"Really, there's a lotta stops between Connecticut and Atlanta. That ass ain't gone be able to walk right when I'm done," bragged Mark.

"I'm ready then, baby."

"You betta be," said Mark.

Shasta grabbed her handbag and her gifts and put them in the truck. Mark grabbed his Louis Vuitton duffle bag that he had pre-packed off the table. Swagged up, he jumped in the truck and kissed Shasta on her cheek.

"I see you were already packed for real, nigga."

"Yep, I told you, I already knew you were going to be my wife," replied Mark.

"Wife?"

"Yeah, wife," said Mark as he reached in the glove compartment and pulled out a Burgundy box with and gold ribbon tied around it. So G'd up, he gave her the box and told her not to answer until they got to Atlanta.

Shasta opened the box and saw the two carat platinum engagement ring set. She didn't waste time putting it on either.

"Yes! Yes! Yes!" said Shasta so excitedly.

"What the hell, the worse that could happen is we get fucking divorced," laughed Shasta.

"Naw, we gone be straight. Plus, you like this dick," replied Mark.

"Fuck you, nigga…with yo' arrogant ass," joked Shasta.

"I will."

"Always and forever…I'm gone be fucking you," said Mark.

Staring at her ring, Shasta reached over and kissed him on the lips before they pulled off. They rode off headed straight for the "A" and leaving the bullshit behind them. A new beginning is what they both were looking forward to. Hand in hand, Shasta watched her past slowly start to disappear in the rearview mirror. She was looking forward to building a new life with Mark and her son Lil' Chris. She was truly happy and Mark was too.

The End

We'd like to thank you for supporting G Street Chronicles and invite you to join our social networks.
Please be sure to post a review when you're finished reading.

Like us on Facebook
G Street Chronicles
G Street Chronicles CEO Exclusive Readers Group

Follow us on Twitter
@GStreetChronicl

Follow us on Instagram
gstreetchronicles

Email us and we'll add you to our mailing list
fans@gstreetchronicles.com

George Sherman Hudson, CEO
Shawna A., COO